I WASN'T SUPPOSED TO WIN, BUT I REFUSED TO LOSE

Lois Williams

ISBN: 978-0-578-81594-7(Paperback)

Publishing Consultant Courage Molina

Edited by Kirsten Quick

Front cover image by Alicia D. Moss | Moss Girls Photography

Book cover design and interior layout by Olivia Heyward | OH Creative Boutique

First printing edition 2020.

DEDICATION

This book is dedicated to my 4 reasons, Mya, Alijah, Noah, and Micah mommy loves you guys!

TABLE OF CONTENTS

Dedication iii

Introduction 1

Chapter 1: My Story A Recipe For Disaster 5

Chapter 2: A New Door Opens 23

Chapter 3: Let Me Help You Change Your
Thinking And Transform Your Life 39

Chapter 4: Finding Your Inner Strength 53

Chapter 5: Grow Your Confidence 69

Chapter 6: Take A Break Selah, Just Don't Quit 83

Chapter 7: Believe in Yourself 99

Chapter 8: Go For It!...115

Don't allow fear
to be an excuse.

Introduction

Dear Reader,

Before you get into the meat of this book, I want to explain how and why this book was written. This book is not a project that I put together in one day. This book was therapy for me. As I poured words out onto these pages; I released years of bottled up emotions that once held me captive. I thought I would never be free of them. To be honest, I have never been completely transparent about my life, mainly because of fear. Fear which has caused me to spend most of my life under the misguided instruction and leadership of my emotions. For as long as I can remember, I have wanted to be a better person, yet I held onto my anger. Anger is what kept me going, or so I thought. It took me a long time to pick up the pieces and get to a place where I was consistently moving forward in my life. However, the fight to become who I desired to be proved to be almost impossible.

Eventually, I reached a point where I could be realistic and transparent with myself. I was able to identify that what I experienced in my childhood and teen years played a major role in who I had become and how I learned how to handle situations in my life.

I've always known that I was created to help people. It is my passion. For a long time, I helped everyone but me. I was amazing at giving advice, but when it came to applying it to my own life, it was a disaster.

Hiding from my past and suppressing the things that had tormented me, caused much damage to me later in my life. When I had finally gotten to the point of desperation, I was able to accomplish things I never thought I could.

As you read this book, I encourage you to challenge yourself. Be ready to make permanent changes in your life and be willing to do the dirty work to make it happen. Don't worry about being selfish as you work on yourself. Don't let anyone or anything distract you from your purpose. Like me, don't allow fear to be an excuse.

This book is an autobiography of my life. My hope is that by reading my story you will be encouraged along your own journey.

Discovering yourself will change you in ways unimaginable! There will be many highs and lows along the way, buckets of tears and days you want to hide from the world. But once you really take a look at your life vulnerably, you will reach a freedom you've never experienced before.

Being an orphan changed the direction of my life. I was raised by my grandmother and left to manage my own pain of my parents abandoning me. I became a teen mother and survived a very difficult relationship.

If you are willing to apply yourself and do the work, you will be able to live your life on your own terms and experience freedom like none other; like I have been able to achieve through my own journey of discovery.

I suggest journaling as you read this book. Write about your feelings, fears and hopes. Your journal will become a reference as you are challenged by circumstances and people in your life.

My mission in sharing my story is to help you realize you are not defined by past decisions and misfortunes in your life. You are able to create your own happiness. The value you add to the world is immeasurable and I want to help you become the best version of yourself! Thank you for allowing me to be part of your journey.

The value you add to this world can only be added by you. You are uniquely you. Stop hiding and dimming your light. There is no manual to how we should live. The only thing you are responsible for is becoming the best version of yourself possible.

Your Author,

Mrs. Lois Williams, LPN

CHAPTER 1

My Story A Recipe For Disaster

As a child, my life was a mystery; specifically, who I was and where I came from. My mother and father were not in my life consistently. Honestly, I didn't even know who my father was. And with my mother, I saw her sporadically for awhile but most of the time it seemed as if she didn't exist at all. No one talked about her or had anything nice to say about her. As I grew up, time moved on but the complexities of my life became more real to me but at the same time made no sense.

My mother gave birth to four children; yet she wasn't a mother to any of us. For the majority of my childhood and well into my teen years, I adorned frustration, confusion, bitterness and pain like clothing. I wanted to know why my mother wasn't there for us. My mother may not have been there, but my grandmother, nana, was. You'll be hearing more about my nana in my book. I'm thankful she took care of me when my mother couldn't.

The Hard Truth

Eventually I would learn the hard truth about my mother. I will go into detail later, but I want to give you a quick summary of why my life never seemed to make sense to me.

My mother used to babysit for her kids occasionally while my nana went to work. I know, usually it's the other way around, but not for us. One day my nana went to work and left us at home with my mother. On this particular day, my mother left to go to the store and never came back.

Even writing this as a 35 year old woman, it still brings me to tears. Even though I didn't know it at the time, looking back, I can see that God was intervening on our behalf. My nana stepped up and raised us as her own.

My life started to unravel. I had been abandoned.

I had absolutely no idea what was ahead for me. I felt unsafe. And no one ever asked what I understood about my mother and father. I was left to imagine where my parents were and what they were actually like because no one ever talked about them.

Although their absences were life altering and heartbreaking, I craved a relationship and connection with my mother more than my father. Maybe it was because she carried me for nine months in her womb. Why wouldn't she have a desire to parent me and nurture me? For a long time, I was told she was 'not all there in the head,' or that she was 'slow' and 'suffered from mild mental retardation due to complications during her birth.' I had no idea what the truth was and no way of truly finding out. This void in my life over the years allowed abandonment, rejection, fear, and compromise to take hold.

Much of the pain I was experiencing was rooted in the fact that the one person I had a direct connection to had no desire for me.

My mother was completely out of our lives for more than two years. I didn't know if she were alive or dead, if she ever thought of me and my siblings, if she had a new family, nothing.

Then, after being absent from our lives for so long, my mother shows up at nana's front door randomly and without notice.

There was never an explanation, an apology, remorse or new beginnings. We, oddly, resumed as if she had never left. It was strange how we avoided everything in my family. No one ever had anything to talk about until a fight broke out. The convoluted truth always came spewing out of emotion, anger mostly.

I was told things about my mother that didn't add up. Even though she abandoned us, my relatives led me to believe that I should feel sorry for her. What or who could ever take precedence over her own children?

I was very skeptical as a child. I questioned everything all the time. I was scared and sad. I craved a mother who would cook me dinner, do my hair... you know, regular mom things.

One great reward for desiring a loving mom is that it led me to the Lord. I prayed daily for my mom to come back for good and love us.

Damaged Goods

The Sordid Details

I had a difficult adolescence. The seeds of disappointment and unforgiveness had taken root. Every decision I made bloomed from those damaged seeds. I craved to be recognized, valued and appreciated. By the time I was 24, not much had changed. I may have gotten older but I was still that sad, scared, abandoned little girl. I was a prisoner in my own life; committed to a life sentence. If my mother couldn't love me then who could?

One day, when I was 10 years old, my nana decided to share the specifics of how she got custody of us. One by one, as very small children my mother started giving us over to my nana for more than an overnight visit. Before I was even in the picture, my nana had raised my oldest brother from the day he was born. Nana was the first person to hold him when he was born. She was doing everything for him as if she were his mother.

After a couple of years, my mother was pregnant with my sister. Nana was already working and taking care of my big brother. My mother only kept each of her children for short periods of time. Her maximum time of tolerance with each one of us was close to two years. It was not long before she dropped my sister off at nana's because she was not able to manage any longer. I don't blame nana for being angry and reluctant about having to raise all of us. After all, she placed her entire life on hold. My nana took on the responsibility of raising and protecting us the best way she could. She was already raising two of my mom's children when I was born. When I was a toddler, my little brother joined his siblings in the 'abandonment club.' At this point, nana was overwhelmed. I'm thankful her love for us was able to carry her beyond her breaking point. She never gave up on us.

The Day My Mother Walked Out On Us

Let's revisit the day my mother left us. Nana received a call from her friend who worked for the Division of Youth and Family Services. She told nana that her daughter had called to open a case. She wanted them to come pick up her children.

It was definitely God intervening that nana's friend got the case and was able to give my nana a heads up on what was happening. Although, to this day, I will never understand why my mother made that call.

My nana left work and immediately went to file papers to start the process of getting custody of all four of us. We became wards of the state at that point. This is when my mother left for a very long time. We did not hear from her or even know if she was alive. No one ever talked about it. Every once in a while someone would ask about her, but there was no sensitivity toward me and my siblings regarding her abandonment.

Nana refused to let us go into the foster care system. She did everything she could, changed her life to provide for us. And to this day, I am forever grateful.

At this time, I struggled terribly with the fact that our mother gave up on us. Did she ever feel love for us? I do know that God loved us because He placed us in our nana's care. I love my nana, but being raised by someone who is not your mother is a hurt no one should have to experience.

Suffocation

As a child growing into my teen years, my hurt had developed into strong unhealthy emotions. These emotions dictated just about every decision I made. I don't know if anyone really knew how deeply I was wounded. My anger and attitude were my only defense. There was a war going on inside of me and it seemed as if winning in this life was impossible for me. It became increasingly difficult to believe in myself. I craved success in so many ways that I learned to fight for approval no matter how I got it. I wanted to be recognized, valued, and appreciated. If I didn't get the recognition I thought I deserved, my bad attitude and behaviors screamed desperation. In the middle of my anger I was always waiting for her. Longing for her. I wanted her to fight for us. She never did. Eventually I lost hope for a happy future. I was like a seed planted in red clay. No hope for blooming. I was suffocating.

My Father

When I was 10 years old, nana asked me if I knew who my father was. It was when we were taking a ride uptown. Nana needed to go to the store, and of course we were always ready to jump in the car and go. We pulled up to the corner store and parked. I asked to go in with her in case there was something I wanted. I remember seeing a woman walking in behind us. There was an uncomfortable awkwardness. The woman looked at me as if she was studying my face. She and Nana did not exchange words just looked at one another. We were done shopping and headed back to the car. Once in the car nana asked me if I knew who my father was? It was such a bizarre question because no one ever discussed my father with me. I was nervous and didn't know how to answer. I reluctantly answered, 'yes.' Nana asked how I knew? I told her when we lived on June Road, I remembered seeing a man walk by the house every day while we were outside playing. He carried a bottle in a brown paper bag. He also kept another bottle in a bag in his back pocket.

It was the way he looked at me. Even as a child, I knew he was my father. This man that never uttered a word to me. I just knew. After this conversation nana and I never talked about my father again.

One day almost a year later, I met my aunt, my father's sister. There was a quick introduction and in no time I was attending sleepovers at her house and playing with my little cousin. Initially, I did not ask questions because I was happy to have someone want to be with me. Eventually, I would find out, the plan was for me to formally meet my father.

Meeting my father officially was very awkward and uncomfortable. There was no formal introduction. I seemingly went from being fatherless to all of a sudden having a father. My father had an alcohol addiction and that took precedence over everything else in his life. I searchingly looked into his eyes for love or for a promise of a better life. But all I saw was emptiness and glossed-over eyes from years of alcohol abuse.

I never wondered why he couldn't care for me. It was almost like I let him off the hook because of his addiction. I never held him responsible for not choosing me. After all, how could he? But with my mother, it was a different story. There never seemed to be a legitimate reason for her dramatic, and abrupt departure out of our lives. Many days I asked God why this was my story. All the cards were stacked against me. I had a mother who chose the streets and men over her children and a father who was an alcoholic.

My Childhood Reality

As a child I had no control over anything in my life. I was forced to deal with it and do my best. I knew if I could make it to adulthood I would prove everyone wrong. As long as I can remember, there was a stigma attached to me and my siblings; that we wouldn't amount to much in life. As a child, that is a very heavy burden to bear. We continued to grow up with not much conversation and a lot of discipline.

I was born with the gift of gab, unfortunately, that was more of an annoyance than a gift to people when I was a kid. No one really wanted to hear me. If I had a dollar for every time I was told to be quiet I would be a billionaire by now. My dad's family let me spend the night and even took me on a few trips. I looked forward to the weekends away from the memories and sadness I had lived, breathed and slept in at nana's. As a child, I didn't have the vocabulary to adequately explain all my feelings from the roller coaster of my life.

The older I got the more I distanced myself from my father's side of the family. Growing up, I was beginning to see the realities of my life clearer. I had come to the realization that it was a choice for both my parents to not want me or my siblings. I daydreamed for years that one day there would be a knock at the door and someone would explain that I was switched at birth. I craved to belong to a household full of love and compassion. That day never came. My life was the perfect recipe of disappointment, sadness, weakness and vulnerability.

Teenage Lens

My teenage mindset had gotten very damaged from all the years of trying to make sense of what had gone wrong in my life. I had no idea how toxic my thoughts had become. My future was a mystery to me.

Love?

At 16 years of age, I met the father of my children, Peter. Prior to meeting him, I had never been involved with a man. To say I was a prude would be an understatement. I was beyond prude. I knew nothing about having a relationship or being intimate. I was a virgin; but the desire to be wanted by someone, anyone, created a corrupted need to compromise myself. I started seeing him secretly, and kept it quiet until I couldn't any longer.

He was almost ten years older than me. He had a job and seemed to have a sense of what he wanted. I was still in high school with a false sense of reality. It did not matter to me that there was such an age difference. All I knew was this relationship was what I had been yearning for. Someone was finally paying attention to me. That being said, no one could have told me this relationship was not compatible.

In the beginning, prior to becoming pregnant, the playful times or the trips to Burger King seemed more than generous; after all, no one else had given me this much attention. I craved more attention, and I became willing to do whatever he wanted because I refused to let him walk away from me. What he wanted was sex. I wanted him to stay, so I gave him what he wanted. It worked for a very short period of time, until we were no longer a secret. I was not able to hide the truth for very long. I loved him and would do anything for him. Things got complicated.

One day when I was at his house, I was sick and vomited the whole time. He was very attentive. Looking back now, I do not know if he was just nervous or genuinely cared about me being sick. It was probably a little of both. I made it through the long exhausting day of being sick. The next day I was perfectly fine. Confusing for me. I went back to school and everything seemed back to normal. The next time we had sex he looked at me and told me I was pregnant. I laughed! No way did I think this could be true.

Months passed and we did not discuss it at all. He did not seemed worried about it. I was still having a menstrual cycle so I just ignored every other sign because I could not imagine myself with a baby. Facing the truth would mean exposing myself and my irresponsibility. For four months I kept my secret until I began to show and people started asking questions. It was not real to me until I went to the doctor's office for a checkup and the doctor congratulated me. I was 17 and almost four months pregnant. Somehow I hid it until my 18th birthday. I knew that if people found out before I was 18, he could be in a lot of trouble. Or at least that was my understanding. Realistically it would not have mattered because I was still a minor at conception.

My Child

Looking back at my decision, I can honestly say that it was very immature. Four months went by and my child received no prenatal care. It was very strange how Peter and I never talked about the baby. It wasn't a priority. It did not even seem to matter. Peter went on with his life as if every day was just a normal day. We still slept together but we never talked about the pregnancy. At this time I was still living at home with nana.

I knew I had to break the truth to my nana but I hadn't yet. I had a conversation with Peter's sister and her husband and they said I could stay at their house if anything went wrong with my telling nana the truth. One day while nana was at work, I placed my car registration and keys on her nightstand. I knew my car would be the first thing to go when she found out I was pregnant. Nana returned home from work that day and asked my sister why I put my car keys and registration on her nightstand. My sister told her I was pregnant. I never got to tell her myself.

This began the longest and hardest journey of my entire life. Nana packed up all of my things and put them outside on the driveway in the rain. I had hurt and disappointed her beyond measure. Firstly, because I hid the truth from her, and secondly, because she wanted more for me. I was at the point of no return. I could not imagine having an abortion or giving up my child. After all, I was the child that was abandoned and rejected by my own parents. Even though I felt inadequate and incapable, I made the conscious decision to love and take care of my child. I never wanted my child to feel the way I felt as a child.

I moved in with Peter's family. I had hoped for the best but it was a very uncomfortable situation. I would soon learn that this pregnancy had greatly affected both Peter's family and my own enormously.

My Pregnancy Getting Real

I was finally going to have the opportunity to give all the love that I had bottled up inside of me to someone else. I didn't know how I was going to take care of my baby but I wanted the chance to do it and prove everyone wrong. At the end of the day, all I really craved was to love somebody and to be loved. I was so very ashamed but at the same time, felt such love.

Going to school became very difficult. I fought the condemning looks and accusations. I battled through the gossip and losing friends. Being a pregnant teenager and falling under the stigma of 'being easy,' was a burden that I carried for a very long time. I was an honor roll student prior to this. I went to school. I did my work. Sadly, even before I was pregnant, I always felt it wasn't enough. My family just saw me as my mother's child. I'm not sure if they expected me to succeed or fail.

I was a teenager who was pregnant by a man ten years older than me. I fiercely wanted to protect Peter and my child. Back then I never even considered the fact that Peter was an adult who pursued a relationship with a teenage girl. My relationship with Peter was the same until the baby was born. I gave birth to my baby boy, Alijah.

The Tides Turn Again

It was a weekday when everything changed for me. We were on the way to pick up the baby from one of my friend's houses. She was babysitting while I was at school. I called her to let her know we would be picking up baby Alijah. She told me she wasn't home. She happened to be at our mutual friend's Alex's house. He and I were friends as well and I had been to his house before. Little did I know that while I was on the phone with my friend, Peter started getting very angry with me. He asked me if I had been to Alex's house before. I said I had because he was also a friend of mine. Before I knew it, I felt a sharp sting to my face.

That was the first time the abuse happened. I was in shock. I didn't know what to do. All I could do was cry. Why did he get so angry? This incident commenced to even more or many more years of further physical abuse. I never talked about what was happening between us because I loved him. I'm not sure if anyone in our lives knew what was happening. No one ever asked or talked about it.

One time when I had a black eye, nana asked me about it. I told her I hit it on the corner of the car door. She didn't believe me. She said, 'Yeah, ok. Keep letting him put his hands on you.' She walked away and it was never discussed again.

I would be so careful to figure out what to say and not to say to Peter. I failed repeatedly. I thought, if I loved him harder, if I did more, it would help him change. I knew he had his own demons. I felt for him. I loved him. Helping him find happiness and purpose became a topic of every prayer conversation with God. Ultimately, I knew that what was happening between us wasn't all his fault or mine. We were both products of our past. Two halves do not make a whole. Our relationship was off and on for years. By the age of 22, I had three children with him. I compromised so much of myself for the sake of my children.

You Can't Love Abuse Away

It took me a long time to realize that no matter how good I was to Peter, no matter how much I loved him, I couldn't change him. If Peter didn't want to change, he wasn't going to change. However, I did want him to be happy, healthy and whole for the sake of our children. It was a hard lesson to learn but I had to come to the realization that I wasn't going to be able to love him back to life. The reality I had yet to face was that at some point I was going to have to leave him. But I didn't think there was going to be any kind of life for me outside of him. I knew the situation. I could navigate this situation and I just couldn't see life without Peter. What would I do without the chaos? I didn't know what normal was. What was normal?

I neglected everything about myself that I knew to be true to chase after a reality that was never even a probable option. I put myself in so many vulnerable situations. I failed to see the truth, which in turn, created difficulties with identifying what was even true. I was so broken and damaged that I had become numb to life. It didn't even matter to me what happened. I was existing in life and not living. I just needed to get through the day and for years that is all I did. I became good at just existing. At some point, the only thing that made sense was to keep moving forward and accept whatever happened. Life had beaten me down so much at this point. It seemed as if no one truly understood me at all. I didn't understand how this had become my life. Why had I put myself through this? Why was abuse okay? I functioned as best I could. I worked and took care of my children. All I wanted was to be wanted by someone, anyone. I could not seem to find it. I had given up on being happy and settled for satisfied. I didn't even need genuine, I just needed to feel something other than what I had been feeling.

Eventually, I turned to alcohol and promiscuity. I just didn't care anymore, nor did I want to feel anymore. I knew that things were getting pretty bad when I stopped caring about going to work and had started drinking more and calling off work. My life was out of control and I didn't care. I begged God for years to get me out of the dark hole that was my life. I could not see anything outside of the struggle. I wanted a fighting chance. There had to be more outside of what I had been living through. At this point, Peter and I had joint custody of Alijah and Noah but there was no agreement concerning my baby at the time, Micah. See, when I found out that I was pregnant with Micah I was only two weeks along. I was working at the hospital when I found out that I was pregnant again. Of course, Peter and I were not on the same page nor were we on good terms. Even so, I called him from the exam room and told him that I was pregnant. He didn't want me to have the baby. He said, 'You know I don't want any more children.'

Things got really crazy after Micah was born because Peter literally functioned as if we only had two children together. He wanted nothing to do with Micah. It broke my heart because beyond all we had been through something in me still believed he could be a good father to our children. So I started raising Micah full time on my own and we shared custody of Alijah and Noah. It wasn't easy. I was literally dropping the oldest two off at his house and having to pay someone to watch the baby when I had to go to work. The heartache that I experienced was traumatizing. To again love someone who didn't have the capacity to love me back broke me in more ways than I can account for. Things got so bad that there were days that I didn't want to live anymore. The pain felt physical, the heartache was so overwhelming. In a perfect world, my childhood would have been perfect and the life I dreamed of with Peter and our children would have been picture perfect. It just didn't turn out that way.

A New Beginning

One particular evening our church was having a men's service with a speaker. Even though I was messed up and broken, the church was the only place that provided peace for me. I went to the men's service this particular night. The men of course sat closer to the front of the church and the women sat behind them. I remember looking around at all of the men in the church. My heart ached for my children. I put my head down and cried. I begged God to give my children, my sons, such examples. I knew Peter had it in him but was unwilling or not capable of giving that much of himself to them. I really felt like I had failed them beyond repair. As I sat there I put my head down and just prayed. As the preacher was speaking, he stopped and started prophesying. My head was still down and I was just talking to God. He then called me to the altar and gave me a word. I had never met him before but the way he spoke into my life about my life, I knew it was God. The people I had grown up around had never spoke to me like this. For the first time in forever, I felt as if God had finally thrown me a lifeline. At this point, I was willing to do whatever it took to live and not merely exist. Someone finally saw me. Don't get me wrong, he didn't give me a word of prosperity. He could see my pain. He spoke to the concerns I had for my sons, and how I felt I had failed them. He also spoke to the fact that I did, in fact, have a relationship with God.

A few days later, I reached out to the preacher and sat down with him. I met with him and his wife. I remember him asking me, 'What would you do if God moved you somewhere where you didn't know anyone?' Nonchalantly I responded, 'I guess I'd be moving.' Little did I know, just a few months later, that conversation would become a reality.

For years I knew I needed to leave New Jersey, but fear gripped me, and kept me planted in the chaos that was my life. After my meeting with the pastor, I started to become more optimistic about the possibility that there was actually a better life for me, somewhere other than where I was. So in August, unbeknownst to me, an opportunity for a trip out of state came up. A distant cousin offered me the option to come visit her in North Carolina for a couple of weeks. I was more excited about the opportunity to see someplace different, so I accepted her offer.

I will never forget the feeling that came over me the day I walked out of the airport onto the curb as I waited for her to pick me and Micah up. It was euphoric, literally. I felt the weight of everything I had been through lift off my shoulders. I could breathe for the first time in what felt like an eternity. I had no idea what was ahead, but the opportunity felt good. Over the course of the next two weeks, I fell in love with the idea of freedom. Freedom from all of the negativity and drama that had become a way of life for me. While I was in North Carolina, I attended church with my cousin. I was introduced to her pastor and he gave me a word about my life, my struggles and relocating. It blew my mind because it was parallel to the word I had gotten from the pastor in New Jersey, and I knew they didn't know each other.

That for me was my confirmation that God was speaking to me. I made the decision to relocate to North Carolina. I wanted to give my children a better life.

CHAPTER 2

A New Door Opens

My trip to North Carolina had been nothing short of amazing and eye-opening. During my stay, I was able to see the city and get a feel for what my everyday life could be. Some days I drove through the city looking around. At that point in my life, anything would have been better than living in New Jersey. I had never been anywhere prior to getting on a plane to North Carolina. When I landed in Charlotte and stepped outside of the airport, I felt an immediate sense of relief. It was like a weight had been lifted off my shoulders. For years, I had felt as if I had been walking with a limp and bent over. I could now stand up straight and breathe. This was where I needed to be. It was after my two-week visit, which went so fast, that I knew I needed to change my life. I had been so miserable and depressed that I didn't want to live. It was bad. I had prayed for change and this was my chance.

God was answering my prayer. I had many questions and reservations. My reservation was fear, simple as that.

Now I was faced with the reality of having to make some very challenging decisions to produce positive change in my life. When I had gotten home from my trip there was no question that I needed to move away.

Nothing had changed in the relationship between Peter and I, but I still needed to talk to him about my decision to move. The excitement about the prospect for a better life overshadowed my fear and anxiety once the plan to relocate was set in motion.

The Courage To Move On

At this point, Micah was a little over a year old and his father had never spent any time with him. While we both had joint custody of the oldest two children, there was never a formal agreement pertaining to custody concerning Micah. With the custody agreement, I couldn't take Alijah and Noah, but I could take Micah. I didn't want to separate the children when I moved.

It was such a struggle because when my mother left us with nana, my nana never allowed us to be split up, no matter how much she had to struggle. I cried and prayed incessantly and really leaned into what God was showing me to do. I wrestled with God. I remember as I was packing up Micah's clothes to go to North Carolina, God told me that Micah shouldn't come with me; that he should stay with his brothers and father. Peter agreed to keep Micah.

My plan was to move to North Carolina and get settled and then come back for the boys. Initially, everything seemed as if it was going to work out. It appeared that we had finally agreed on something for the first time in a very long time.

Time To Go

I will never forget how broken I was the night before my departure. Peter came over to my apartment and picked up Micah along with all of his belongings. I remember changing Micah's diaper for the last time. As Peter walked away, I watched Micah's face. A small part of my heart was satisfied because I was seeing something I never thought I would. Micah was in the arms of his father. I believe, despite our issues, Peter loved his children. Even though I was broken and sad, I knew it was temporary. I was comforted by the fact that my boys would have their father and grandmother to care for them while I was away.

I drove to Peter's house before I left to say one more goodbye to my children. Afterward, I went to my best friend Amy's house to spend my last night in New Jersey. Amy was my person. My sister. She had seen me through many broken days. She cried with me and lifted me up. Her family had been like my own for years. We always had each other's back. I left New Jersey at 3:00 AM.

I remember saying goodbye to my dear friend. Outside on her driveway we hugged and cried. I was going to miss her more than words could describe. I probably would have stayed if she had asked me to. She was the ying to my yang. I was leaving without my children and my best friend. What was life going to be like? I cried during most of the drive to Charlotte. The excitement of the move was the farthest thing from my mind. What was life without the struggle and responsibility of providing for my children? That's all I knew.

Charlotte

Once in Charlotte, I'm not going to lie. I struggled. For months I fought to find a smile. I knew I was where I needed to be, but I still couldn't function. I had no idea who I was outside of being a teen mom who struggled to provide and care for three small children. The unfortunate pattern of existing had followed me to North Carolina and was very much alive in my life. I remember one day I went to church and someone said to me, "Ok Lois, you have got to pull it together. You have to start caring about yourself and what you look like." I was so sad. Most days, all I could manage in self-care was putting my hair in a ponytail. Not having my children with me had pushed me into a deep depression. My existence was rooted in depression. My emotions were my driving force. I had learned how to live by being guided solely by my emotions.

Another Turn

Thankfully, I gained the strength to climb out of my black hole. After several weeks in Charlotte, I secured a job as a medical assistant working at a doctors office. I knew that through this job, I could earn the support I needed to bring my boys to North Carolina. I began to focus and plan for the future.

Unbeknownst to me, Peter had a plan of his own. It wasn't long before he stopped answering the phone. And it was nearly impossible to get in touch with him. Peter eventually made it very clear to me that he did not intend on moving the boys to Charlotte.

The tables had completely turned. Before I knew it, I was petitioned by the court for custody and child support. This sent me straight into a panic. Even after many phone calls to attorney offices, there was no resolve. I couldn't afford a retainer fee. I had to look for attorneys while I was at work. I would go into the bathroom and make phone calls. I was in the bathroom on the phone feeling so defeated with tears running down my face as another lawyer wanted $5,000 for a retainer fee.

Thankfully, God spoke peace to me and said, "It won't take all of this." A sense of reassurance engulfed me and I hung up the phone immediately. At this point, I still had no idea how God was going to work this out, but I trusted. I was hurt and confused. I wanted my boys. I only left them because I didn't want to disrupt their lives.

For almost a year and a half, Peter had made it virtually impossible for me to be involved with my boys. It had even gotten to the point that I was ordered to pay him child support. I was ok with that because they were my responsibility as well. It was unfair, however, because Peter had refused to pay child support when I had custody of the boys.

Long Days

And so it began. Every week the child support was taken directly out of my check. For almost a year and a half I was back and forth to New Jersey from North Carolina for court. I won't lie, every time the judge declined my request to move the boys to North Carolina, it felt like a 'Never.' I couldn't stop fighting though. My faith was stronger than my doubt. God told me I would raise my boys in North Carolina, and that's what I held onto.

Many times during my trips to New Jersey, he wouldn't even allow me to see the boys. Some of the visits I would have to get the police involved. It was all so inhumane. The police could not order him to give me time with my children because it was a civil matter. I couldn't grasp why Peter was trying to punish me.

Every time the judge would delay the case and reschedule another appearance, I followed his instructions and went back to North Carolina and did everything he said I needed to do. Although I was frustrated with the entire process, and even more upset with God, I still had to fight for the boys.

I fasted and prayed. I laid on my face and cried out to God. Fighting for my children was the hardest fight I had ever faced. I was fighting for our life together. I had only survived as long as I had because of my children. I missed everything about them: crying, making bottles, changing diapers, giving baths, and putting them to bed. The tasks I had once found tedious, I now craved. I couldn't imagine a life without my boys. So I continued to fight. Fighting was all I knew. This was my opportunity to fight for a purpose. I was fighting for something bigger than myself. I wasn't fighting to alienate the boys from their father. I was fighting to give them a better life.

A life much better than the one I knew growing up. I wanted to give them a life with definitive answers. I didn't want my children to have to guess or wonder about anything, if I could help it.

But I was exhausted. at this point I had been spiritually, mentally, emotionally, and physically in a fight for what was right for the boys and it drained me. It took my faith and the faith of my church family to pray me through and build my strength, especially on the days when I just wanted to give up. There were even days when I thought maybe the boys would be better off with Peter's family. He could actually give them a family and that was something I couldn't give them. But God just wouldn't let me settle. So I continued to fight and drove the ten hours from North Carolina to New Jersey for court.

In The Midst Of The Fight

The disappointment I felt after each court appearance became more and more unbearable. It became increasingly more difficult to cope with because I wanted us to share custody, and Peter wanted to take the boys away from me.

I was tired of driving all that way and then back to Charlotte in defeat. I wanted to cry most of the time. There were many times throughout the process that I questioned where God was? It was unimaginable that God would leave me to deal with this by myself. We were back and forth to court so much that we took the case to trial.

The date for the trial had finally come. I was again a ball of nerves as I drove back to New Jersey. I was so fearful as I arrived at the courthouse. Up to this point, it looked as if I did not have a chance. Throughout this judicial process, I had so much to fix and prove before I could have a chance at getting my boys. Here's where things got complicated. The day before trial, I lost my job. The job that had the benefits and means that would allow me to take care of my children. As we sat before the judge, he questioned the both of us in regards to caring for the children. The judge then asked me for proof of health insurance for my job and at that point I almost lost all nerve. The crazy thing was the day I lost my job was the day I had received the insurance cards in the mail.

I really began to panic because I had lost my job. The judge reviewed the insurance cards and decided they were proof enough of my ability to take care of my boys. Originally, the judge would have had his clerk call my place of employment to verify coverage. But something has gone my way!

My heart was beating out of my chest! I was so relieved; however, the case wasn't closed. The judge still had a decision to make. The yes or no came down to this one man. But I trusted God. I had my faith.

The judge gave us a lengthy speech before he retired to his chamber to deliberate and make his decision. He recessed for an hour. It had to be the longest hour of my life.

As soon as I walked out of the courtroom to wait, I immediately sent a group text to everyone from my North Carolina church. I asked them to pray because the judge was in deliberation. Soon the recess was over and we were back in the courtroom. The judge looked at us and said, "These cases are never easy, I had to make a decision today that Solomon himself couldn't make." At that point my heart was at ease. I put my head down and the tears began to run down my face. That was God speaking directly to me!

His final decision was that I could move my boys to North Carolina with me. I was bringing my babies back home.

My Kids And A New Beginning

I was nervous when the day came to pick up the boys. They were always my babies, but I hadn't cared for them in over a year. So much had changed about them. There was a lot to learn about them. They were so big. It was always in the back of my mind that they would be mad at me because I had not been there for them.

Life with dad was completely different from life with mom. If this move was going to be successful, I knew I had to take my feelings out of the decision and trust what God had told me. The one thing I had prayed throughout the entire time I was separated from my children, was that God would redeem the time. My prayer was that the boys wouldn't know how long they had actually been away from me.

For them, God delivered just what I had prayed for. When we were reunited it was as if no time passed. They hadn't forgotten who I was to them. The challenges we faced were with behaviors and discipline. If I had to label the way I parented versus the way their dad parented, it would be good cop versus bad cop. I was the one who laid down the law and expected them to follow directions on a daily basis. For Peter, he disciplined them when he reached his limit. After being away from me for over a year, the fight to incorporate structure back in their lives was very taxing. They didn't like to follow the rules. They fought with each other, and no one knew how to sit down. Although I was beyond excited to have them back with me, at the same time, it was overwhelming. From single life back to caregiver. No time to pout or take breaks. I had to adjust back to mommy mode. I asked God for this and He delivered.

I really wish I could say it was all peaches and cream and that everything was perfect. It wasn't. Getting the boys back and living in a new state was one of the hardest times of my life. It wasn't days or months, but rather years of adjustment. Originally, when the boys moved to North Carolina, the custody agreement between their father and I included us splitting holidays and summers; which meant I had to bring the boys to him and he had to bring them back to me.

After awhile though, Peter stopped responding to me about transportation for the boys. If I didn't drop them off and pick them up, he wasn't going to be involved. Walking through this with no solid support system of my own brought many complications into my life. Even though I had been through hell and back with Peter, deep down I still loved him. I still longed for him to get his life together and be the father he never had. The both of us had come from broken homes. Life for us growing up was less than favorable. We had both become products of our environments and upbringing. No matter how weak I felt, fighting for a better life was all I knew.

Now that I was not drowning in my toxic environment, I was able to dream and work for a better life. I felt safe enough to acknowledge everything I needed to become the mother my children needed. I wish I could tell you that life was great and we flourished, but that is far from the truth. I was struggling to repair myself and still be adequate in terms of parenting and raising my children. I struggled with the fact that I had failed to give my children a two-parent home with parents that loved and respected each other.

Time To Grow

I committed my life to getting to know God. I wanted to come out from under all the years of bad elements and situations that had plagued my life for so long. I fasted and prayed and laid on my face and cried out to God. I needed to be vulnerable, but I was so fragile. My church family was all I knew. They allowed me to vent and have meltdowns until I regained my strength. I finally felt like I had a safety net and it was okay to be broken; in order for the pieces of my life to be put back together. Slowly but surely I could see that structure and discipline were being established in my life. But years passed and I had become complacent and fearful instead of fearless. I was so tired of struggling to make ends meet. We were never on the streets and we never went without. Although I did not have everything at that time, I had enough.

Thankfully, one day an opportunity presented itself to me by a special woman in my life, Sheila. We had been introduced to each other through church, and God used her to open a door for me that put me in a much better financial situation. Shelia was in human resources at her company and when a customer service position opened up, she helped me apply and get the job. Finally things were looking better. Over the course of about six years on the job she became my confidant, counselor, and prayer warrior. She always made me see the glass half full instead of half empty! I worked as a customer service representative for almost six years.

The job was steady until one day the bottom dropped out. I found out I was being let go. We were all told in November of the impending January layoff. After fasting and praying, I decided I would go back to school and complete my nursing license. This was a very hard decision to make but it came down to making the decision to struggle and sacrifice short-term to reap a better life for me and the kids. So I decided to go back to school. I committed the loan amount a month before school started. I knew this temporary financial setback would set me up for a permanent come back.

Going back to school was absolutely hands down the hardest process I had ever experienced. I used to tell people all of the time that I would rather give birth three times over without any pain medication than to complete nursing school again. I had applied to an accelerated nursing program which was fourteen months long. It truly felt like an eternity. I kept telling myself, "one day at a time." Throughout the entire time I attended school I was stressed. I could not work for almost the first nine months and my children lived alone like bachelors. I had no help but I prayed that God would keep us while I made this sacrifice to give us a better life.

The boys were real troopers but were still children who did childlike things. There were days I couldn't even get upset with them when I came home and something else was broken or messed up. After all, I was unable to be home to parent them, so it was what it was. Many days I saw them in passing only. I meal-prepped for them and taught them how to use the microwave thirty seconds at a time. Eventually, I secured a job at a pizza store. One of the pastors at my church was a district manager for the company and he got the job for me in one of the stores conveniently near my house. I was closer to finishing school and needed to bring income into my household.

I started making pizza and negotiated with one of the owners a higher hourly pay if I took on more responsibility. So in less than three weeks, I learned how to make everything on the menu and was running shift. Soon after, I became a closing manager for more pay. Most days at this point, I was in school all day and saw the boys in passing as I changed from school uniform to pizza shop uniform. While I worked, I would have my books open on the counter and studied when I could. I was determined not to fail.

Finally, after months of sacrifice it was all coming together. I don't think my children were mad about eating pizza every day for a few months. I kept telling myself that all I needed was my nursing license and we would be okay.

I Did It!

It finally happened for us. I received my nursing pin on April 16, 2016. The sense of accomplishment I felt after pinning was euphoric. Now I had to study for the nursing boards to receive my license.

I studied for my nursing boards for a month. I tested May 2, 2016. The nerves and stress I endured for forty eight hours after the testing was insane. I did not sleep for the two days that I had to wait. I interviewed for my first job May 3, 2016, and accepted my first nursing job that day! The very next day, May 4, 2016, I received confirmation that I passed my boards. I was now a licensed nurse.

My license was official on the North Carolina Board of Nursing website on May 11, 2016. Five days later, May 17, 2016, I officially started working as a nurse. In just a month I went from living off $1,500 a month, to making over $2,000 every two weeks. It felt like we had hit the jackpot. Life moving forward would never be the same for my children and I. We had survived so much. I was finally able to provide my children a better life. I could not only afford their needs but their wants as well.

My life was going in a much better direction. Even though I was now successfully working as a nurse, there were still instances when I struggled with the 'what is next' factor. I had to force myself into a better headspace. When you come from a life of trauma, you expect a negative situation right around the next corner; that at any moment something bad is going to happen and disrupt life. We can get so caught up on what could be that we forget to celebrate what is. If I was going to continue to move forward, I had to realize and recognize that things had finally changed. This change was not temporary, it was permanent.

Every day, I had to dig deep and encourage myself. I had to stop comparing my success with the success of others. I had evolved as a mother, and as a career woman. My identity was finally more than just a teen mother. I had truly beat the statistics!

A Healthy Mindset

I began to live as if all my other dreams were on their way to me. I was walking by faith. So I began to live as if everything else I had dreamed of was on its way to me. It is called walking by faith. You have to find your reason for pursuing your dreams. What is your why? What is the reason you have to go harder? For me, it was and always has been my children. In spite of my many failures and setbacks I was determined to show them a better life.

I don't ever want them to experience what I did as a child in terms of sadness, disappointment, neglect, abandonment and fear. I finally stopped punishing myself for the situations where I felt I had failed. I started celebrating my successes no matter how small they seemed to everyone else. The pressures that once plagued my life had been dissolved. I could breathe, smile, laugh and love myself freely. I was no longer abusing myself behind the scenes. I learned to be open and honest and move forward positively. My mindset had everything to do with being able to move forward and accept that things had really changed. I had finally learned to accept my success and live a life of faith beyond my fears, faults, and flaws. I was finally a woman evolved, and it felt so good! Having a healthy mindset is everything. You can have a good life but if your mindset is plagued, you can not see what is clearly in front of you. To be successful and happy, you must change your thinking!

CHAPTER 5

Let Me Help You Change Your Thinking And Transform Your Life

T rust me, I completely understand how crazy it sounds to say, "Change your thinking." I can certainly tell you that the process of changing the way you think, and the way you see things, will be far from an overnight fix. However, I can tell you that it is definitely possible. It will take a lot of practice, correction, and hard work. You will have to acknowledge every fault, flaw, and shortcoming.

We must take responsibility concerning our actions instead of running away from them; and continuing to place the blame on other people. Most of the time it is easier to blame the way you are on someone else. Just remember, the more you free up your heart and mind from the negative, the more you can make room for the positive things that will come. This process is very painful but the more you come to grips with your reality, the sooner you can heal from the inside out. Let me tell you, it will never matter how much money you have, or how successful you become, if you don't do the work you will never feel fulfilled.

For years I blamed my mother for every shortcoming I had. It was her fault. After all, she left me. I didn't leave her. It was easier for me to blame her. To blame my mother meant I could have been perfect, had it not been for her.

I needed to own my issues in order to correct and become the woman I've always wanted to be. I also needed to recognize that my issues and hangups did not define my future. I decided to take control so that I could set myself free and live the life I was meant to live. A life without boundaries with limitless opportunities. Being able to think clearly allowed me to see life from a totally different realm. I was finally free; free to be the person I was destined to be before the world caught hold of me.

Dear reader, start telling yourself that you can do it! If you do not believe that you can, then you never will. Try waking up with a winning attitude in the morning. Stop allowing yourself to sleep on your frustrations, only to wake up each day feeling more defeated than the day before. Life can be very challenging but change starts in your mind. If you can take control of your thoughts, that power will flow effortlessly in every other component in your life.

You will still have tough days. You may even have days where you consider giving up. It is all normal. These will be the days you have to take a step back and challenge yourself. You may become frustrated or overwhelmed. It is okay. Take a moment and gather yourself. You are the master of your own thoughts and moods. You do have control over your own self. Your emotions do not control you. You control your emotions. Many times, our lives are controlled by how we feel, and not based upon the facts concerning our lives.

Growth comes when we can acknowledge that our feelings are temporary. We don't need anyone else to validate our feelings or actions. Most of the time we look for confirmation through other people. There was a time in my life when I could not make a single decision on my own; from what I wore to how I did my hair. To me, my own opinion was not valuable. I don't even think I believed I had a viable opinion.

So often, we allow our insecurities to dictate our fate. Before I could make a decision to move from one state to another I had to see that more was possible. Now I will say that of course, this was not an overnight change. For years I accepted defeat and despair as a way of life for me. There was not much I could do about my childhood. I had no control over what was or was not. However, as an adult, it was up to me to make a change. I blamed everything and everyone else for my shortcomings and failures. It really did not matter what the circumstances were, I blamed everyone else.

I understand that none of us are perfect. Beating yourself up is not the answer. I should know, I did it enough. Give yourself a fighting chance at success. No matter what it may be that you secretly desire in your heart, you can live that desire out loud. You just have to believe in yourself. You got this!

My goal with being transparent in this book is not to showcase certain aspects of my life; neither is it to make anyone look bad. The reality is we all have our own issues to face. Every person in my life, good, bad or indifferent has played a necessary role in bringing me to where I am now. I have set myself free.

At some point, I had to stop blaming my mother, Peter, and anyone else for the way that my life has turned out. I challenge you to do the same. Take ownership and stop leaving your destiny in the hands of others. Most of the time, to be completely honest, we have empowered people and they don't even know it. The people we have blamed our life's problems on have moved on with their lives. Yet we are still stuck and indifferent, merely existing in life. Now is your opportunity to not just exist but to thrive. Live life on your own terms, controlling the outcome this time around.

Are You Ready To Change Your Life?

Someone helped me to see clearly. Now I want to help you. Stop being hard on yourself. Sometimes we are so hard on ourselves we don't leave room for improvement. We expect failure and disappointment. We put ourselves in compromising positions. You cannot afford to keep wallowing in your misery. It is time for a change. I hope you are ready!

I remember a time in my life when I did nothing but speak and think negatively. I learned to expect people to fail me. There was something on the inside of me yearning to be proven wrong. Every time someone disappointed me, it added to the negativity I had been growing for years. I catered to sadness, depression, disappointment, rage, anger and any other word that identified me as a victim. After all, I didn't make myself this way, life did. Remember, it is impossible to change the world around you.

If you feel that people are avoiding you, or you are being excluded, it may be that the negativity around you is so draining, other people feel it and are avoiding your stress.

If you are really looking for a change, it starts with you. Stop looking for other people to make the decisions that you need to make for yourself. You have to change the way that you think. It starts with what you speak. You have to expect greatness in order to walk it out. Before you can speak it, you have to believe it in your heart. I know for the longest time all I saw was drama in my life. I think my heart started to become necrotic. I did not care what anyone else thought or felt.

My sad truth was that I hated myself. I did not like going home where I would be alone and forced to listen to the thoughts that plagued my mind for years. Again and again I'd become angry and frustrated that this is who I was. I reeked of anger. I wore every negative emotion you can imagine like a perfume.

The bible says in Matthew 12:34 "**O generation of vipers, how can ye, being evil, speak good things? For out of the abundance of the heart the mouth speaketh.**"

Life happens; but at some point we need to assume responsibility for our own life choices. As children, we don't have much control over our lives. The adults in our lives call the shots. But at some point when we grow up and mature, we need to step up and take responsibility for our lives. Change direction and stop the blame game.

The things that happened to me after my mother left had nothing to do with her. She was nowhere to be found. I thought had she stayed we would have been better off. It was difficult facing the reality that whether my mother stayed or left wouldn't have changed anything in my life because she was incapable of being a mother.

The truth is my mother had some learning disabilities due to her premature birth. It was not until I was well into my twenties that I accepted this very real fact about my mother. If I was ever going to move on in my life I had to deal with my heart issues. If I didn't, everything that came from me would come from a place of darkness. I needed a change. I did not want to be negative all of the time. Negativity was all that I knew. But it could only change if I changed it.

Positive Choices

Whenever I talked and a negative statement came out of my mouth I became accountable about the negativity and I would rephrase it. This was a process that I adopted and still use today. Sometimes when I am around people and they say something negative, I am quick to put a positive spin on it. I finally understand that we have to speak what we expect. Think about it like this, if every time you spoke what you expected and it actually happened, how powerful would that be. It is very important to avoid certain words and phrases when you are talking about yourself. Don't start a sentence with "Cannot."

The words or statements we speak, whether it is about you or others, as well as what you hear, turn into thoughts that quickly transform into behaviors or emotions. It is not wrong to have feelings that may be less favorable, or even to express them, but how you express what you think will determine the direction of your thoughts. For example, instead of saying "I am broke," say "My funds are temporarily low." That shows your level of expectation. Speak what you expect with confidence no matter what your situation looks like.

Start replacing negative words with positive ones and watch your outcomes turn around. You will surprise yourself. This is not easy to do but it is definitely worth it. Stop using words that affirm defeat and failure. Learn to incorporate words in your vocabulary that open up the potential for growth, change, and development. Let me give you a real-life example of how what you think can damage what you expect; which is why what you think, speak and expect must be in alignment. I have worked very hard for my career in nursing. The problem I face often is not all nurses seem to care the way I do. That is hard for me to understand.

For me, nursing is a passion and a dream fulfilled. One of my first jobs as a nurse, I took a job with a company and it was not long before I was looking for a way out. I could not stand going to work every day doing what I loved but being miserable. I disliked the way the staff treated each other and the patients. At that time, my speech was a clear reflection of the frustration I felt. Over time, my negative thoughts about where I worked and the people I worked with outweighed my positive attempts for change. It got so bad that I started to speak what I felt and the negativity spread like wildfire.

At the same time, I couldn't understand why nothing I tried was working. The reality was that I allowed my emotions to control what I spoke. Eventually, it did not matter how good I was at my job. The disgust I felt on a daily basis eventually manifested in my attitude at work and my presentation. I stopped caring about how effective my interactions with people were and started showing up just to collect a paycheck every two weeks.

I could share positive phrases or statements, but the truth is I stopped believing in my heart that change could actually happen. I started to say daily how much I hated my job and did not want to be there. I continued rehearsing, "I am not going to quit. They will have to fire me first." The problem was I really wanted to make a difference but it appeared that I was the minority. When it was all said and done I lost my job. I didn't do anything to cause me to lose my job but because of my attitude and how I handled myself at work, I had misrepresented myself. I made it easy for them to terminate me.

As angry as I was, I was also relieved. But I was no longer in the position to produce the change I had once desired. I had allowed how I felt, dictate what I spoke, and that produced a less than favorable outcome.

It would have been so much easier to place the blame on everyone else. But because I knew that I had grown, changed, and developed, it was important for me to acknowledge where I had dropped the ball. No matter what happened, even in an uncomfortable situation, giving up control of my process was a no go. I was not going to allow the work that I had done to better myself be undone.

In order to change our thinking from being negative, we must change what we affirm in our life. We have to be able to see better instead of worse. Stop repeating what did not work. Start evaluating what did not work and look for the loopholes.

It's time to be purposeful in your approach. Start speaking what you desire to manifest in your life. Remember emotions are temporary so stop making a permanent decision based upon temporary feelings. Too many times we speak from how we feel, which is what plants the seed allowing disappointment and failure to grow. What you speak will manifest. Why not speak what you want? There is a difference in speaking what you want versus what you expect. For years I struggled with what I wanted and expected. It was like everything was running together. I couldn't tell right from wrong because I wasn't willing to right my wrongs. You can not change your reality if you can not face your reality. If I never came to my senses and changed the way I was thinking, I would have never been able to turn my life around.

One very important thing that worked for me was journaling. For me, writing became my way of escape. Let me be clear, it did not start off easy. Journaling meant I had to be real. If I could not be real on paper, in a book that no one else would see, then that meant I was fake. So I started to write. I wrote about anything and everything that came to my mind. I just needed a release. I could put on paper the thoughts I couldn't express to anyone else. I could be real and free in this one place called my journal. In order for me to be able to change my thoughts, I needed to free up my mind and express what was on the inside of me.

I had to be vulnerable. I was desperate. Desperate enough to go to the worst places inside of myself and do the work to clean it up. There is something freeing in the fact that I could be real with myself.

If we aren't willing to be real with ourselves then we will never be able to be real with anyone. The more I was able put down on paper what I was feeling, the more I felt myself opening up. I noticed that once I was able to get through the darkness in my life, there was actually light inside of me. My vision about myself and the world around me started to change. I wasn't just a little girl that was abandoned by her parents; a child who was rejected and abused. I was a grown woman who was facing her issues and evolving.

I decided to do the work and figure out who I was and what I wanted. I could finally see more for myself and my children. If we can't see better for ourselves, then everything attached to us will start to die. I did not want that for myself or my children. The reality is we all have issues whether they are from our past or our present. No one is perfect. You have to see that for yourself or moving forward will never be an option. You too can do the work. If you're reading this book then you are certainly on the right path and right page. It's time to do the work and fight for your life because you matter. It is important to learn how to operate outside of how you feel. Don't be driven by your thoughts or emotions. Every time you open your mouth to speak, it should be of substance and value.

I want you to understand that everything you have been through has brought you right where you are now. It hasn't been a waste.

There is much value in disappointment, fear, hurt, anger and sadness. Pain produces power. It's up to you whether it will be a negative or a positive power in your life. How can you go through all you have and not fight for what you want?

Write down in a journal or on a piece of paper what you want from life. It doesn't matter how big or small. Put your expectations out into the universe or in a prayer journal. But you have to begin to write and rehearse positivity. Most of us have spent enough time reliving the past and every negative thing, that we unknowingly have poisoned ourselves.

It's time to change your thought patterns. You have to fight like never before to reverse the damage. Don't panic. It is doable. It will be just fine. Before I was able to thrive in life, I spent a lot of time sinking in my own despair.

Let me be clear, up to this point, a lot of the decisions that we have made have been decisions that threatened to take us to a point of no return. Not being able to see life from outside our own point of view caused us to be selfish. From all of the pressure and pain, we may have become reckless. This is the time to turn it all around. No longer allow your pain to influence you to do things that will only jeopardize your mental health and well being. My relationships and connections were based upon the need for approval from other people.

It is time that you start to love yourself enough to free yourself. Beyond every issue. You deserve to live a full life. I most certainly hope that at this point you are starting to feel more optimistic about what is next for you. I promise you, the options are unlimited. Years ago, if someone would have showed me where I am now in my life, I would have called them a liar. No, it hasn't been easy. But once I got sick and tired of being sick and tired, I became desperate enough to fight for change.

Not only is it important to change the way we think by reversing our thoughts from negative to positive, but most of the time our toxic relationships were formed with our toxic personalities. There are definitely some relationships that will not survive this next phase of your life. Understand not every intention is a good one. There are some people who are connected to you because of what you have or can offer to them. Some connections have absolutely nothing to do with you just being you. The truth of the matter is that many times we connected ourselves to people just to occupy empty space in our lives. Doing so definitely created diversions that kept us from dealing with the issues that kept us stagnant for so long. Some of these connections run so deep that they will cause you great pain to let go, but know that disconnection is necessary.

Don't be afraid to let go of relationships that are detrimental to your growth. Stop begging people who have chosen to walk away from you, to stay. Whether you realize it or not, you are doing more damage to yourself. I can certainly speak for myself when I say I spent years chasing people and begging people to be around me. It nearly broke my heart.

There are people that I thought I could not survive without. These same people who once walked the same path in life with me, went another way. For a long time, I punished myself when relationships in my life did not work, until I started to acknowledge that there was value in who I was. The more I could see my own worth, the easier it became when people walked away or when I had to let go of a relationship. It may not seem like it now, but I promise the right connections cannot form until you sever the wrong ones.

Who you're connected to can have a major effect on your mindset about life and how you see yourself. Some of your relationships have made you compare yourself to them time and time again. These same relationships have birthed self-pity and self-doubt in your life. One very important lesson I learned was how to create boundaries and stick to them. You teach people how to treat you.

Stop allowing life to become more complicated for no reason. Think about it like this, if someone worked for the secret service and quit or retired, she no longer has the same clearance she had prior to the change. There are guidelines and limitations moving forward for her. Well, the same holds true for friendship and relationships, and the changes you are making in your life. Decide who is necessary to be in your life, and put people in their proper places. There are people who are meant to be in your life for a reason, a season, or a lifetime. Do you know who belongs where? The problem that I continued to run into was that I kept trying to make my reason people seasonal and my seasonal lifers. Stop allowing yourself to be mistreated because of a troubled past. We deserve better. Stop begging people. Just let them go. It is time to give space to the endless opportunities that are opening up because you deserve better.

Let's put this chapter in perspective. You will overcome and you will move forward. In order to successfully change your thinking, you will need to apply three very important principles. The first principle is to start telling yourself that you can do it. The second one is to write down the things that you want and begin to live them out. Finally, it is imperative that you disconnect yourself from people and situations that have become pillars of negativity in your life. If you truly want more then now is the time to get it. Stop short-changing yourself.

Everything in your life is not bad. Take a step back and evaluate where you are right now. Sometimes we can become so caught up in what is wrong that we fail to acknowledge what is right. When was the last time you celebrated what was going right? Stop erecting your issues and breathing life into them. The key here is to start. You have to start in order to get moving.

Nothing good can happen if you refuse to align yourself with purpose. Your process is hinged upon your willingness to put in the work. I promise you this, if you are willing, you will not fail. I don't care what it looks like or how long you've been down. Pressure produces power so don't fold yet. Everything you've been through is about to make total sense but you will never see it if you give up. Anything worth having is worth fighting for.

CHAPTER 4

Finding Your Inner Strength

Hopefully, by now you are feeling more optimistic about your life and what's ahead for your future. Prior to picking up this book, you may have felt helpless and hopeless but I believe and pray that as you continue reading, you will find even more strength and self-awareness with each flip of the page.

I want you to make a promise to yourself: never again give up. Settling is no longer an option. Understand that even though life is going to keep moving and things will happen, you are strong enough to handle whatever comes your way! I don't care who gives up or walks away from you. It is important you understand that you do matter. You are much closer than you think, literally one step away. This may be the hardest step. It is a step of faith.

You'll have to leap forward into purpose and destiny! As long as you are willing, there is always an opportunity for positive progression in your life. Yes, you are a winner! Nothing is impossible if you believe. All of our belief systems are different. I am a Christian. My hope is that no matter who or what you believe in, that you trust in yourself.

By this point, you have learned that the first step to a better future begins with how you think. What you feel, and how you progress all depend on your strength and ability to see past the forest to a green pasture and a better future. I am very excited to be on this journey with you. As I am writing this book, I am experiencing every emotion imaginable. If I can help just one person, this book will have done its job.

Faith

Faith is on the other side of fear. That is the real power! You can overcome fear by faith. You are a powerhouse. It's time to get plugged into the Source. Cars can't run without gas. Lights won't shine without electricity. The television remote will not work without batteries. I think you get my point. If you are feeling weak or drained, take a moment to plug into your power source.

My power source is God. He gives me the strength and courage to reach my goals. "For who is God except the Lord? Who but our God is a solid rock? God is my strong fortress, and he makes my way perfect." 2 Samuel 22:33

You are still reading, so this means you are ready to gather up your inner strength. I promise you have the power to pull yourself together. Dig deep and reach down within and speak life into yourself. Tell your own dry bones to live. As a child, it was my blind hope that helped me. And as I grew up, I felt weak because I started understanding my circumstances. Feeling weak is a very vulnerable and powerless place to be.

It was very challenging to fight against the odds that seemed to control everything about my existence. I had no control over what happened to me. Once I became a teenager, I couldn't seem to get anything right. I was weak and I was moving through life slowly like a snail. It felt like I was stuck in slow mode even though life was speeding by.

After I became an 18 year old mother, it felt like the weight of the world rested on my shoulders. Moving seemed almost impossible. However, no matter how heavy my life felt, stopping was never an option. If I stopped, who would care for my kids? I wasn't living. I was existing because my children needed me to.

Nowhere To Go But Up

Can you identify with feeling so burdened mentally, emotionally and even physically? Well, just know you are not alone. It is not the most comfortable feeling, but you can make it. I was so weak and defeated at times that it almost felt like not living would be much better than life. When I hit rock bottom, I knew there was nowhere to go but up. I was at a point in my life when I knew whatever was ahead of me was better than what was behind me.

The more I tried to depend on people for my happiness the more depressed and oppressed I became. The reason people failed me was because I allowed it. The truth is I put my trust in the wrong people and things. You can not afford to continue to give people control over you. Take responsibility for the choices you make for yourself. It is time that you have a say in the way things will go from here on out.

Self-Empowerment

Don't leave the decisions up to anyone else. You are in the process of growing your confidence and regaining control over your life, and that my friend is beyond exciting! It is vitally important that you understand that you may not come out on top every single time, and that is okay. Failure is a part of growing. The power in moving forward with confidence and in control means that you will be confident in making decisions no matter the outcome. Learning to depend on yourself is a process. For me, that was difficult.

I was always telling people that I couldn't depend on anyone but myself. The truth is every decision I made in my life was ultimately based upon someone else. I did not make decisions based on what I wanted to do. I made them based upon what I couldn't do. I wanted to be safe. Staying within the parameters I allowed in my life made me feel safe. But the more comfortable I became in that life, the more uncomfortable my life became. Does that make sense? I knew I needed to feel more than safe. I had built a box around my life. A fortress. But I wanted more. Needed more.

I was born to be different. We all are. I did not need to depend on people to live my best life. I realized that to survive in this world, I needed to acknowledge that I was strong enough and good enough. Many days,the weakness and inadequacy I struggled through threatened my peace of mind. I am here to assure you that there is power in your ability to push through. You have to see yourself as victorious. Even on your worst days.

Everyone Has A Breaking Point

Have you ever seen the show "My 600 Pound Life"? If not, please watch it. I relate deeply to the people that struggle in this show. This show is about people who have allowed fear, doubt, weakness and sadness to dictate their lives. Sound familiar? In the show, these people are on the verge of physical death. They are living a life where they are trapped, not just inside their own bodies but in their homes as well. These people stopped living life for themselves a long time ago. Many of them deal with shame behind their choices. They eventually reached a point where they found the strength to change their lives. Just like I did. Just like you will too.

Let's rewind for a moment and let me be transparent with you. The relationship I had with Peter, the father of my children, was predetermined long before it actually started. Initially, I thought I knew it all. From my point of view I really thought I was the one in control. What I would ultimately learn many years later was that control was never mine.

I knew that the possibility of getting pregnant was real. However, when I actually became pregnant at 17, I had absolutely no idea what to do. I did not think anything through in regards to how I would handle the situation if it actually happened. What I did know was that if it did happen, I would prove to everyone who had abandoned me in my life, particularly my mother, that I would be a better mother than she was. That thinking did not serve me well. I was seeking revenge instead of a better life.

One child led to two which eventually became three by the time I was 22. All because I had a point to prove. And it became a prison for me, much like the homes of the people on that TV show. For a long time, I couldn't see a way out. For years I struggled with depression. I had no desire to live anymore. The only reason I made it through the worst seasons of depression were because of my children. I didn't want to give them a life of uncertainty, the life that I had experienced with my parents. What is it in your life that will ignite the change that you need to make?

The people in the show, "My 600 Pound Life," had health scares that fueled their internal strength to make a change. Providing a better life for my children was my motivation to change my life. That and being plugged in to my power source, which is God, gave me what I needed to change my life.

I learned that I couldn't depend on other people who could ultimately fail me, especially when my children depended on me. Learning to trust myself was one of the hardest things I've ever done. However, I had no other options but to pull myself together and lean on what I knew.

After a while, it actually became invigorating to be able to make my own choices. The more in control of my life I became, the more I found power in my ability to make a choice.

Trust Yourself

How do you learn to depend on yourself? It is not very complicated, but can still be difficult. Learning to depend on yourself starts with trusting in yourself. Stop looking for others to confirm your choices. The choices you make will have a direct effect on you and your life. You live and learn from the outcomes. Every decision you make along your life journey of self-discovery will not always be right or the best decision. But find your inner strength. If you truly desire to make a change in your life, it starts with finding courage. Courage to make a decision and be okay with the outcome. The more you lean on your own understanding, you are watering the seed within. Your courage and persistence will develop. Over time you will start to see how much easier it is to make decisions and feel secure in them.

No one makes all the right decisions, and if they say they do they are lying to you. A big part of finding your inner strength leans on the process of soul searching. You will never find the hidden treasures within if you do not dig deep.

It is time to do some soul searching! During this process of looking within yourself do not seek understanding from the outside. It may seem easier on your most challenging day but stay the course. Remain focused on your goals and priorities. I can assure you that you will not lose. I challenge you to make time for peace and quiet in your day. It doesn't matter where that quiet place is, just find it and get there. One thing that helped me when I felt the most bottled up was to write everything down. Sometimes you can't understand your feelings until you see it written out. Write it out. Everything you journal will not always be pretty. This is your opportunity to be completely honest with yourself. I don't care what comes out. What I care about is that you understand your poor choices, and that your circumstances do not define your future.

"He determines the number of the stars; he gives to all of them their names. Great is our Lord, and abundant in power; his understanding is beyond measure." Psalm 147:4-5

I did not have time to wallow in every part of my life when I was at my worst. That's where my faith in God led me. The great thing about God is that He kept me strong. He allowed me to manage and function enough until I was able to make it to a safe place in my life. You will be unable to understand the truth about yourself and your inner strength if you aren't willing to put in the work. We will no longer give credit, whether it is good or bad, to anyone else in our lives, for the outcome of choices we make ourselves.

You Can Do This

Freedom and strength will come once you assume ownership over your life, and the choices you make. Just like it is better to own your own business rather than spending all your time building someone else's. The same is true in reclaiming your life and finding your own independence. Not just physical independence, but the most important, your emotional independence. Without emotional stability and independence, you will always feel inferior, not just in regards to people but in life.

For many years I could not see anything that was right about who I was or the choices I was making. I made all of my decisions based on what everyone else thought or wanted me to do. For me, it was easier that way, or so it seemed. I lived my life in a fog for years. My mindset was so clouded with doubt, fear, and dark thoughts.

The relationship I had with Peter had been very toxic for years. It wasn't until that one terrible night in his car, with a double sided blade at my throat. That was the night it all changed. I knew I had to do something. This was not going to be my life. I had to live. I had to do better for my children. I don't want to bash Peter. He had his own issues long before me. I was not okay with how he treated me. It's a blessing that I have reached a place in my life where I am able to forgive him. It is a burden released.

Honestly, I felt my strength was in him needing me. I wanted to save him. But when trying to save him could have killed me, that changed everything for me. After that night, I decided I would no longer live for the sake of other people but for me. I had finally decided to stop living my life on someone else's auto pilot.

Making My Own Choices

Somehow I mustered up the strength to get my life on track and focused. I was finally willing to work on fixing myself. Can you identify with living in a fog and merely existing day in and day out? Feeling empty and struggling with the simplest of decisions? I remember one day needing to go to the pharmacy to pick up a calendar for my purse because I was on my new path to self-discovery. It literally took me 20 minutes to decide on one calendar. The calendars were all the same. The only difference was the picture on the front. Talk about anxiety!

I spent so much time giving everyone else in my life control, that I never learned how to make even the smallest decisions on my own. But everyone has to start somewhere, and for me, it was right there in the pharmacy. After I finally made the decision on which one I would buy, the freedom that I had gained in that one small choice was exhilarating.

Stay with me. Whatever makes you anxious, big or small, you can push through it. There is power in the push through. Faith is on the other side of fear. It takes one step in the opposite direction of where you have been traveling. Keep reading, we are on this journey together. This book will be a situational aid for you. Meaning, no matter where you find yourself, this tool will serve as a guide.

I am sharing my real life examples. Yours will be different. Either way, the principles you are learning will guide your success! You've got this. If you haven't heard it lately, I want to remind you that you are strong and powerful. Your life is worth living on your own terms. Understand that everything you have been through has been worth it and necessary. Be open to your process. You will feel stronger! I've been right where you are. Thankfully, my strength continues to grow.

Dig Deep

You may feel burdened under layers of life on top of you, emotionally. Think about it like this: before a flower can bloom, it has to be pollinated. Before a butterfly can grace this earth it begins as an odd looking chrysalis. Before a seed blossoms into a plant, it must break through the soil. There's a process before all these things evolve into what they were created to be.

Unlike nature, we are able to think. I believe that if we can think it, we can achieve it. It all starts with a plan. We have to be able to push through all of the disappointment in order to come out on the other side.

Tell yourself that tomorrow will be different because you are making a choice right now. Your confidence has always been there. It has just been tucked away, until now. Soul searching is like spring cleaning. You get to dig through all of the old stuff and sometimes find stuff you thought you'd lost a long time ago. Things that you couldn't put a value on.

Your inner strength is priceless. As you continue to read this book, I hope your strength will continue to grow! Allow yourself to be engulfed in this process of rediscovery. I promise everything you've gone through and survived can help someone else someday. Stop pitying yourself and asking, "Why me?" Instead, ask, "Why not me?" The more you can fight back against the negative thoughts and stop breathing life into negative self talk, that is the minute you win the battle. You need to see yourself as the person you desire to be before it can come to pass. Begin to set small goals of self-discovery. Find the things that really matter to you and begin to invest in them. Figure out who you are and where you really desire to be in life. Remember, there is no age limit concerning self-discovery or locating your inner strength. Success doesn't possess an age limit. You have to cast down the negative thoughts you speak toward yourself. Sadly, We often assassinate ourselves before anyone else even has the chance to.

Where do you start? Let me break it down like this, using school as an example. Most of us begin our school careers in preschool or pre-kindergarten. We may start in the same place but our individual journeys may look very different. Each of us were tested along the way in order to be promoted to the next grade level. We did not always pass every test along the way and some of us were held back. Although we may not have enjoyed school, it shaped us educationally. Life is no different. Every year we develop, reach milestones and continue to evolve. In school, there are students who pay attention and earn extra credit and study meticulously.

Most often, these students become high achievers in society; the people who commit to the hard work no matter what. Failure is not an option for them. On the other hand, there are also students who do just enough to get by. These are the people who are okay with mediocrity or settling; not pushing themselves to achieve more.

Decide now which path you are willing to travel. Your decision will determine your dedication as you continue this journey of learning your way to a better, healthier you.

The hardest decision I've ever made was leaving New Jersey and my children to move to North Carolina. This was a journey of self-discovery that I knew I had to make. I had to trust God and my process if I was ever going to be free from my colorful past. Something inside of me made me believe that there was more on the other side of it all! The closer I came to North Carolina, the freer I felt, mentally and physically. Although I was sad and missed my children, ultimately I knew this time I would not quit because I was never going to fail my children. I want you to understand that as you take back control of your life, everyone will not be on the same page as you.

Pruning your Relationships

I have been emphasizing the importance of finding your inner strength. Before you can connect to the new you, you must disconnect from the old. As you are in transition you will most certainly face periods of isolation. You will physically see people fall away from your life. Let them. But it's not easy. For me, it was very depressing because the more people I lost in my life, the more I craved relationships. But just as a plant or tree grows, it needs to be pruned to cut the dead parts off and to keep growing. We need to do the same in our lives. If the people in our lives are hindering our growth, then they need to be cut out of our lives. It is easier to let go of people in your life if they are not meant to be where you are going. I wish I knew then what I know now. I promise I would have let them go a long time ago.

You've Got This!

I am excited you have made the choice to change your life. There are truly no limits to your change. In summary, change the way you think and tell yourself that you can do it. Write down everything you expect in life and start living it out. Disconnect from all the negative energy that has plagued you for so long. You will start to feel very free when you do this.

By the time you reach the end of this book, you will feel even lighter because your freedom will be on another level. You need to access your inner strength. You are going to become independent; while at the same time, soul searching and finding out who you are and what you want for yourself. You are able to become the best YOU because now you are willing to do the work.

Your mind is the most powerful tool. Use it to your advantage. A strong mind will take you through the 'push through' phase. I know how hard that is. You are moving in the right direction.

Poor outcomes are like bruises. Bruises heal and so do hardships in life. I want to encourage you to drop the experience and take hold of the lesson in it. Too often we hold on to every single experience so it doesn't happen again. When we need to let go and look forward not backward.

Remember, you are the pilot of your own plane. You are no longer riding through life on someone else's cruise control. You are in control of your own destiny. With the knowledge, guidance and right tools, you have what you need to move forward and be successful.

Be brave. Accept your new future of endless possibilities. Take what did not work and turn it around to make it work. I understand we can not realistically redo life or situations; and life continues to move forward at a fast pace. But you can redirect all the years of negative energy. Turn it into fuel. Allow it to propel you forward.

You are in control. Please continue your journey of self-discovery. As you read this book you can either take notes or highlight what sticks out the most. Acknowledge your progression. Don't be too hard on yourself.

CHAPTER 5

Grow Your Confidence

Welcome to the next phase of your growth process! If you had any doubt that you couldn't move forward, you have already proven yourself wrong. Congratulations! As I'm sure you've learned by now, the game of life doesn't stop, no matter how hard it may become. It's important to celebrate the small stuff. It is healthy and wise to acknowledge your successes, no matter how small they may seem. Sometimes we are afraid to celebrate because we feel we are undeserving. It is necessary to acknowledge and celebrate any and every accomplishment in your life. Every step you take in the right direction is a step farther away from your past life. Stop settling for less because you haven't seen more for yourself.

You deserve a new way of life. A life full of real, genuine joy and love. You have to be able to see the world differently. I learned as a child that being positive was uncommon. I was more likely to see negativity and complacency. It was my experience that no one wanted to see anyone get ahead. Everyone was okay with not doing anything. The reasoning behind living that way was that once you start to evolve, and change the way you see life, it forces those around you to take another look. Your transformation will make some people in your life uncomfortable. The reality is that some people were never supposed to be in your life in the first place.

Don't Stay Trapped

Imagine a world of endless possibilities with healthy perception and people to celebrate with. You can create this world for yourself. You get to choose who you allow in your space and for how long. Let me be clear, family or not, that doesn't matter. Most often, it is and has been, those closest to you that won't want you to change. They may try to bring you to those low places you have been fighting so hard to get out of because that's all they know.

I kept Peter in my life even after the abuse started because I saw another person wounded by life, much like myself. I fell in love with his potential. Beyond his faults and shortcomings he was funny at times. It appeared that he needed one person to not quit on him. Who better than me right? Or so I thought. After all, I totally understood what it was like to be abandoned and given up on. What I did not know was the amount of time and years his family had already invested in trying to give him the help he needed. I was incapable of providing the help I so wanted to give.

I failed to see that hurt people hurt people. I did not acknowledge that two halves do not make a whole. I kept changing myself to fit him. I became so fixated on trying to make him a better person that I lost myself in the process. For years, all I could focus on was fixing him and all it did was damage me even more.

Blinded By The Truth

I was told I was pretty and smart by friends and people in my life. My confidence and self-esteem were so low, I could not see it. I was so damaged, I was incapable of seeing what other people saw in me.

How was I supposed to think for myself when I did not trust myself? Instead, I trusted people who continually hurt and disappointed me. People who had proven repeatedly that I was not a priority to them.

When I first found out I was pregnant when I was 17, it was all so much to take in. I was completely naive about life. I think I lived in a false reality my entire childhood. I always thought I didn't have much of an imagination. Later in life, I found out that wasn't true. It's not that I didn't have an imagination, it was just that my way of dealing with things was not dealing with them at all. When I found out I was pregnant, I had been on birth control pills and had been going to the planned parenthood clinic. I was a junior in high school. Peter and I spent a lot of time together. Being pregnant was something I didn't even consider.

Blunt Reality

I had visited the clinic to get my next three months of birth control pills. I was handed a cup to pee in because they always test you prior to prescribing more birth control pills. I had been taking my birth control pills this whole time. Imagine my surprise when the nurse came back into my exam room and told me I would need to stop taking the birth control pills. She told me to make an appointment with a gynecologist because I was pregnant. I was in shock. Peter told me he thought I was but I never considered that to be true.

Well, now it was all becoming real. What in the world was I going to do with a baby? I didn't even know how to raise myself. I hadn't even been in the world long enough to be confident enough to think that I could become someone's mother. I am sharing my story with you because I want you to understand it did not start well for me. My life seemed to be one big roller coaster. My hope is that I can encourage you to keep moving forward. I assure you with all I've been through,I would never believe that I could become a published author. I am now confident that all of my experiences in my life have been for a purpose.

So I find myself four months pregnant. It took me eight pregnancy tests and a lot of nerve before I scheduled my gynecologist appointment. I was pregnant my entire junior year. I tried to hide it the best I could for as long as I was able. My body turned traitor on me. I was changing rapidly.

One day I happened to be at Peter's sister's house and she came right out and asked me if I was pregnant. I was definitely showing way more than I thought. I quickly responded with a 'no.' She didn't buy that response. She could tell my body was changing because she knew me very well. Before I even met Peter, Peter's sister and husband became surrogate parents to me and my brother. We went everywhere and did everything with them. I was with them all of the time. So like any mother who is in tune and paying attention, she knew the answer to her question before she even asked it.

I will never forget the day her husband, who I called dad, took me for a ride uptown to the dollar store. We were walking around and talking and as gentle as he could he asked me if I was pregnant. I started crying and admitted the truth that I was in fact pregnant.

That was a defining moment in my life of what having a father was supposed to be like. That was something I had never known. So the word was out and the news spread like wildfire.

The fact that I was 17 when I got pregnant was the issue. And then finding out that Peter was the father was an even bigger problem. Peter was almost ten years older than me.

I remember how gentle they handled me after I told them the truth. We sat down and formulated a plan on how I would tell my nana. I was so scared. Now, I've already shared with you what happened when nana found out. And I completely understand why she took the news as hard as she did. I knew that in her mind all she would see is another mouth to feed and be responsible for.

After raising my own children, I understand completely that stress. But at that point in my life, I was clueless. After she threw me out of the house along with all of my belongings, she did not want to see me for a long time. I didn't see her until after I gave birth to my son months later. I had my son August before my senior year. I went right back to school in September.

Hard Times Make Strong People

Although life was terribly difficult, something in me kept going forward. I adopted the 'One day at a time' principal, managing each day as it came. I can not even begin to fully explain the level of fear and intimidation I struggled with during this time. The major struggle was mental because I did not have either of my parents growing up. All I was sure about was that I could not and would not fail at being a mother. I had a lot to learn and a lot to prove.

Being a teen mom, who was still attending high school, I acted like I wasn't bothered by the judgement from my friends, peers and teachers. It was my defense mechanism. I was dealing with adult issues as a teenager. I was facing one failure after another, which caused me to dig deeper into self doubt and depression.

Despite my situation, I overcame my struggles. With each day of opportunity, I learned to accomplish my goals. There will be times when you have to stop overthinking, and ignore your feelings to move forward. Many days that was exactly what I had to do. I would have been stagnant if I had spent too much time focusing on what was NOT working for me.

Failure Is A Big Step To Success

A part of developing self confidence is learning to be okay with failure. There are simply some things you may have to fail in order to understand just how to succeed. That statement isn't really confusing once you analyze it. The reality is it's extremely rare that someone can master the art of something without a few unsuccessful attempts. We tend to look at failure as defeat but I want to challenge you to start looking at failure as an opportunity. An opportunity to see where and why something may not have worked out exactly how you expected.

When I went to nursing school I did not pass every test. As a matter of fact I failed a few of them. You may remember in school going over a test and reevaluating what you missed. This is important because we were given a second look into what we did wrong. This is the same lesson with life. Evaluating failure allows us to do something differently the next time.

Failing forward means that even though we may not have been successful the first time, we don't give up and quit. We need to go through the reevaluation process and figure out how to put the pieces back together; to fill in the gaps and see the process through to the finish line.

Growing up, no one ever taught me about failing. I never understood that it is okay to fail as long as you keep moving forward. I felt as if I knew everything I needed to know. The truth is that I knew a whole lot about nothing; and in a short period of time I had to learn a whole lot about everything. I did not have a choice. I had to grow up and mature if I was going to tackle my new role as a mom.

Growth

Having my son Alijah, my first child, changed my life. Even though it was hard and challenging, my confidence as a young woman started to grow. I had to learn to trust myself with him. I had to be confident that what I was doing for him was right. There were times when people questioned what I was doing and almost made me second guess myself. I asserted myself and stood firm on what I believed was the right thing to do for my child.

I know a lot of people can identify with my story because I know I am not alone. The reality is, I had been afraid to share because I wasn't confident in myself. I did not feel as if I had made it far enough to be able to tell anyone about what I had survived in my life. What is important to take away from my story is the fact that hiding it won't help. Whatever it is you are afraid to face just FACE it. Neglecting it won't make it disappear.

I have learned whether the outcome is going to be good or bad you have to deal with the situation head-on. I can look back now and see the many ways I could have avoided so many of the situations I had gotten myself into. Hindsight is twenty-twenty. Let my hindsight be your foresight. You can definitely avoid some of the problems I faced by being open to my story.

Obviously if I had listened to my nana when she warned me what could happen if I slept with a man, I would not have ended up pregnant. I had failed in so many areas up to that point I didn't know what to do. I kept failing until I figured out how to succeed. I got to a point where I learned how to fail forward! I was finally able to see that I was not perfect and neither was anyone else. I began to see the world around me quite differently. I became comfortable with the fact that failing was not the end of the world. Although it was very taxing to have to go back and start over, I was willing to do that and it made all the difference. I finally reached a point where I became willing to fight for success and stop focusing on my issues and hangups.

It is okay that you haven't made all of the right choices and that you have failed at some things in your life. You are in recovery mode now and you can't recover everything if you can't acknowledge anything. It is time that you gave up on that defeated mindset and walk with your head high because confidence is key. When I learned the importance of confidence, that's when things started to come together. It changed everything for me. I could make decisions faster and trusted my decisions. I no longer needed to make a million phone calls to find someone to agree with me before I made a choice. I trusted that I was perfectly capable of trusting myself no matter the outcome.

Wanting To Be The Best Version Of Myself

Because I was not afraid to fail, I was able to take chances. I took advantage of every opportunity to push for a better life for myself and my child. I was determined to not become a statistic. I did not want to be just another black girl from a broken home who ended up on government assistance and never did anything with her life. Let me be clear, I am not against getting help when you need it but my belief is that being on public assistance is crippling for so many people. I didn't want that for my life.

Despite my beliefs, I did end up on public assistance for a while. I received the help I needed to help take care of my child. I did not want to need public assistance for the rest of my life. To reach my goal I knew I would have to work harder. To achieve more in life I would need to be the best version of myself.

Sometimes we have to humble ourselves and utilize the resources around us in order to really be able to take advantage of opportunities for growth and development. I could share many stories about how fear limited my ability to take advantage of opportunities that were right in front of me. I allowed feelings of self doubt and inadequacy to hold me back. I lacked confidence for so long because I could not let go of the fear of failing.

Letting go of fear grows confidence, which enables you to not care what other people think if you fail at something. God is not looking for perfection. He is looking for a willing heart. I was always taught as a child in church that people will judge you based upon what they see but God judges you based upon the intent of your heart.

"... The Lord sees not as man sees: man looks on the outward appearance, but the Lord looks on the heart." 1 Samuel 16:7

Walk with confidence into every decision you make going forward! Stop doubting yourself. Stop living your life in the shadow of endless possibilities and thrust yourself forward. Get up out of self pity, and stop wallowing in self doubt. Those days are over.

You may not have done everything right. And you may have failed many times. So what. You are still here for a reason. That counts for something. This is your opportunity to shift your life into high gear and go after what you've always wanted. The more confidence you acquire, the more self sufficient you become. The more you establish your independence, the more you manage your own decisions.

Who cares what anyone thinks about your personal choices? If you are like me, you may have based past decisions on satisfying someone else. We no longer need to view the world through someone else's lens because we are capable of seeing it for ourselves.

The amazing thing about change, growth, and development is evolution. You are continuing to evolve. If I had continued to listen to every negative thing someone had to say to me or about me I would have never been able to accomplish anything at all. For a long time I gave people more control over my life than I should have; all because I failed to see the value within myself.

You deserve to be happy. We all do! No matter what decisions we've made in life. Make the most of what is ahead of you. Take advantage of every opportunity as if it were your last. That kind of perspective changes everything. Even small choices matter. It is important to start tracking your progress along the way. For me it was very freeing to finally see the things I had envisioned actually happening in my life.

In summary, we are stronger when we tap into our inner strength and understand the importance of it. We need to set boundaries with people so we are no longer codependent and know how to depend upon ourselves. We've started the journey of soul searching in order to gain a clearer understanding of who we are. We also know why we need to push through our disappointment because if we don't, there is no way to successfully move forward.

We will no longer put ourselves down. We will start telling ourselves that we CAN do things instead of we CAN'T. Journaling and tracking progress is important. Better out than in. If you are not comfortable with talking to someone, that is perfectly okay because the paper won't talk back. Sometimes we need to free the clutter in our mind to be able to think clearer, which will allow for better decision making.

Pruning Out Lives

The hardest part about moving forward is resisting the urge to reach back and attempt to bring people along with you. Let me make something very clear. Whoever is meant to go the distance with you in this lifetime will do just that. You will not have to fight to maintain relevance in any relationship. If it is a fight to maintain, then you certainly need to be realistic and evaluate the relationship. People are either in your life for a reason, a season, or a lifetime.

Relationships go through growing pains that will either make it or break it. This make or break depends on all sides not just yours. While you are steadily changing, eventually you will realize how taxing it is to maintain connections with people that you should let go. You will drive yourself crazy chasing people down to figure out what is going on and what you may have done. I know because I have done just that over the years.

I simply got to a point where I wasn't even focused on my own growth because I was too busy trying to keep up with my past while moving forward. I know how crazy that sounds but it was true. Eventually I came to a crossroad; either I moved full steam ahead or I would stay stuck in my past. I came to the decision that my future is more important than my past. I learned to be confident in who I am, and to appreciate the people who want to move forward with me.

Disconnecting from some unhealthy relationships will be very challenging. If we handle the disconnection the right way it will be very beneficial. Sometimes a relationship may have just run its course. Recognize the value in it, keep every lesson you learned but let it go. The right connections can't be made if we hold onto the wrong ones. I would suggest being honest with whoever it is in your life you're making this decision about. I am not sure why people are afraid of closure but it's pretty valuable. You don't have to leave a relationship bitter, you can actually leave it better. Just because it is over doesn't mean it has to end badly.

Just like we discussed earlier, it is ok to adjust to failure. The relationship just did not work out. In some cases you've known for a while that it was over. You are brave and you need to know that. It takes a strong person to go through the things that you have experienced and still be willing to fight to move forward into a promising future. I challenge you to challenge others around you to level up.

CHAPTER 6

Take A Break Selah, Just Don't Quit

There is a big difference between breaking and quitting. Don't let anyone tell you different. Just like when you're driving your car. There's a big difference between stepping on the brakes and the engine failing. When you hit the brakes it causes a temporary pause in the movement of the car. But if the engine fails, the car is incapable of doing anything at all. This example is no different than pausing music versus turning the power off. If you pause your music, you have the option and ability to resume. But if you turn the power off, you can press play all day and you won't hear a thing.

Life is no different. We've intended to pause but we've unintentionally turned the power off. This time around however, you will be more conscious of how you move forward. If you truly desire to function at your highest level and be the best you can, then breaks are necessary. When I was in nursing school, it was actually a requirement that we took breaks after forty-five minutes each hour. We were taught that after forty-five minutes our brains were not absorbing what we were being taught. We needed to physically get up and leave the classroom. It was like resetting our brains.

Many of us would go outside and walk laps around the building or walk the halls of the school. Either way, the teachers would stop teaching for those fifteen minutes. I can attest to the validity of taking such breaks. I returned to class more alert and refocused to continue learning.

Once you establish the value in what you are doing and understand what it will take to accomplish it, breaks are imperative. I wish I had known the importance of breaks earlier in my life, as I wouldn't have become a serial quitter. When something became more difficult, I used to give up. The stress and emotional trauma I struggled with for so long crippled my ability to see clearly. It was so difficult to identify good from bad that instead of taking a break, I would quit.

We most certainly are strong enough to take a break and continue. Sometimes we need to take a break and step away to obtain a fresh perspective. Most of us have had a recipe for disaster in our lives. Catastrophic events can make life seem impossible, and so painful that it's hard to imagine ever feeling like ourselves again.

You are valuable and necessary. Quitting is out of the question. You deserve the best life has to offer. Whatever you've always desired is right on the other side of what hasn't worked for you. This process of self-discovery is all about you. It's what you've wanted but just couldn't find your way, until now.

If you continue to hit the reset button in your life and keep starting over, you will remain stuck. Just take a pause in this game called life and refocus, but come back to it. Sometimes we can get burned out.

No More Giving Up

I thought I burned out many times in my life, where quitting seemed like the only option. I allowed low self-esteem and self-doubt to assist me in forfeiting my destiny. Sadly, I gave up on myself more times than I can count. I would have loved to place the blame on someone else but until I assumed responsibility for myself, life would be a merry-go-round. We will keep revisiting the same issues over again until we take responsibility for ourselves.

You are not who you were and you are more than capable of re-claiming your independence as well as your self-respect. There are more people supporting you than against you. Most of the time the reason we tend to feel alone in our journey is simply that we have placed our focus and expectation on the wrong people. We have placed so many layers of false expectation on people that we thought should be there for us.

Be Careful Who You Let In Your Space

I remember a time when I had a fall out with someone. I placed expectations on this person based on the relationship I thought we had. I later found out that my idea of what our friendship was, was totally one-sided. I ended up having to apologize to her because of how I treated her.

When I got upset, she did not care the same way I did. Once we were finally able to communicate and talk through everything, I was clear on where we stood. I no longer held her to the friend standard that kept me so torn when dealing with her. She was not my friend yet I was hers. There was a huge imbalance. I was not able to see it that way for a long time. I had spread myself so thin. I was trying to be who I thought she needed me to be.

One thing I did not acknowledge for years was that life is about learning and evolving. I was taught how to live in dysfunction as if it was normal. Dysfunction was my normal.

I was never taught how to express myself in a healthy manner or how to have a healthy disagreement. Just because you may not see eye to eye with someone does not mean that you have to deny yourself the right to be happy. You are not required to dislike someone just because you have a disagreement.

This is why it is important to be open and honest with people. You may need to have hard conversations with people you're in a relationship with. Knowing how each of you views the relationship will allow you to properly set boundaries and guidelines for how you move forward. Having a clear understanding will allow you to navigate your feelings about people as well.

Once you have a more mature understanding about relationships, you will begin to live in reality instead of false perception.

In this particular relationship, the truth was, this person did not really like me. She tolerated the idea of me because of what I was able to do for her. Sound familiar? The unfortunate part of it all was that I did not value myself enough to acknowledge what was really happening, even though I was fully aware. This relationship was like a merry-go-round I couldn't get off. I placed a lot of emphasis on trying to prove that we could have a genuine relationship, only to realize it had been a waste of time.

We had so much in common, however she did not acknowledge it. This was a relationship I should have quit and cut off. But time and time again, I pressed pause and returned back to it after the sting wore off. I placed more value in trying to maintain this relationship in my life than I placed in myself.

This was all due to my insecurities and thinking that it was my relationships that defined me. There may be some relationships that you need to close the door on. It is time to do some growing. A garden will never produce a healthy harvest if it is not properly tended to. Weeds stop things from growing and expanding. Sometimes farmers or gardeners have to completely turn the soil over and aerate the dirt in order to make it healthy so they can plant a crop. This process takes a lot of hard work and persistence. You must be committed to this process. you can not start, stop, or pause.

Freedom

Decide right now that you are going to be the best version of yourself. Commit to moving forward. You have to adopt the mentality that this is business and not pleasure. This time, make the decision that is best for you and stick to it. There can be a great level of fear and anxiety dealing with issues from your past. Understand that real freedom is in accepting all of your faults, flaws and failures.

I am finally at a point in my life where quitting is no longer a viable option for me. I do not care if it seems to be the silliest idea. I will try it. I will do my best. I won't know where I could be successful if I don't try.

I needed to stop punishing myself for my past. You need to do the same if you want to move on. People can hide and lie all day. I can assure you that no one has a past that is squeaky clean. Do not worry about how people perceive you. It is none of your concern regarding how others feel about you. I made a promise to myself that I would no longer limit my future because of the inadequacies of my past. I am willing to live in my truth. The truth about who I am and where I came from. The truth about where I failed and the lessons I learned. The truth about what worked for me and what did not. The truth about how I failed myself and why I will no longer be a quitter.

We can not change our pasts but we can adjust accordingly and take control of our future. For many of us, never pushing ourselves and not fighting for more was a learned behavior.

The good news is learned behaviors can be altered. We have to be teachable in order to learn new ways and to accept change. We can not change what we are not in a position to acknowledge.

No Excuses

My mother taught me inadvertently that it was easier to quit than to persevere. My mother didn't take time away as a break or a vacation. When she took time off, she left and never came back. She never reclaimed her role as my mother. She would visit and leave as if she were a mere acquaintance. Even though my mother quit on me and my three siblings, that could not be my excuse for not following through in my own life.

Let me be completely honest. For a very long time, I stayed stuck in a place of misery because I was stuck on the fact my mother gave up on me. I held onto the traumatizing thought that if she didn't see enough in me to stay, how could I possibly see more in myself? I was letting what she did to me define my life.

After a while, I automatically expected and accepted defeat and failure. After all, that had been my experience as a child. As an adult, I felt so hopeless I could not see a way out of feeling like my entire existence was a failure. I would even ask God why I was born into my situation. How had this become my life? A life of just existing. I did not know what true happiness was.

I am not talking about someone who was not accomplishing anything either. I was a perfectionist from elementary school and beyond. My fight to be good at everything came from a deep need for approval from everyone around me. I felt invisible and wanted to be noticed.

You Are More Than Your Past

My family environment seemed to be entirely different from my classmates' home life. I can recall memories as early as first grade when I had received awards for perfect handwriting. I was an honor roll student from elementary school through high school. It did not seem to matter in my family. God gave me a fighting spirit.

There was not much invested in who I was or who I had the potential to become. My upbringing and early life experiences groomed me for my relationships. The letdowns were very painful because of the false expectations I placed on them. I became angry at the world. I wore a false smile like a costume. I learned how to function in my dysfunction.

I was about 23 years old when life started to change for me. At that point, I was so beat down and defeated. I had hit my rock bottom. I felt as if I was walking around with a monkey on my back. At that point, I was a single mother to three children and struggling doing life on my own. It was extremely hard not to want to quit and give up. I did not feel like I had much to offer my own children. How was I supposed to raise capable little human beings when I felt so incapable?

A Better Life

I had reached a point in my life where I was going to live or die. That's when I started to fight for my change. I finally decided that I owed it to myself and my children to try to give them more. I knew that if I did not fight for more we would never get it. I refused to let them grow up the way I did. Knowing how bad it was for me, I finally came to the decision that it would not be the same for my children.

You can reach a place of such desperation in life that it all comes down to living or dying. It's at that point where you make a conscious decision to choose YOU. Choosing ME meant I was choosing life. It meant I was choosing my children. Just because you make this bold decision, it doesn't mean everything will come together overnight. For me, this is where everything took a turn.

If I thought my life was complicated up to this point, I had no idea what lay ahead. All because I made the decision to choose life. To make the monumental decision of leaving everything I knew in New Jersey to move to Charlotte, North Carolina.

The only way to see the entire truth about your situation is to step outside of it and see it from a totally different perspective. If I was going to live and not give up, I had to do things completely different. What I want you to know and be aware of is there are going to be tough decisions that will make you feel like you are failing. It's important to acknowledge that this time things are going to be different. They are different because you are aware of what is happening, of the choices you are making, and that you are in control.

In my past, and maybe yours as well, I made blind choices based upon the opinions and thoughts of others. It is different now. It's time to take responsibility for what will happen moving forward. It will be very important to remind yourself why you are doing what you are doing. You will need to continue to acknowledge your 'why.' What I mean in acknowledging your 'why' is that your 'why' is your reason. Your 'why' may even be your 'who.' Why are you doing this? Or who are you doing this for? I don't care what the 'who' or 'why' is. What I do care about is you know that even on the hardest days you have to keep moving forward.

For me, my 'why' was because I wanted to experience more out of life and give my children so much more. I wanted to be happy. Not just tolerating being a parent, but loving the honor of being chosen to bring such amazing children into this world. There were so many times I wanted to give up during the year and a half my children were in New Jersey and I was in North Carolina.

It would have been easier to give in and let their father and his family raise my children, but I fought to show my kids my love for them and that I wanted to provide for them. Driving over nine hours every month from North Carolina to New Jersey, and not being allowed to see my children or spend time with them was heartbreaking. I could only see them through the glass screen door of his house. It was a struggle to keep fighting for what I knew was right. I was exhausted physically and emotionally. Ultimately, because I learned to pay attention to my process and acknowledge exactly where I was, I started to make conscious and purposeful decisions. I was no longer walking around with my head in the clouds. I was fighting through depression and heaviness to get to my happiness.

'God is our refuge and strength, an ever-present help in trouble.'
Isaiah 41:10

Your beliefs may not be the same as mine. I can only tell you my truth from my perspective. I know for a fact that if I did not have faith and a relationship with God, there is no way humanly possible that I would be writing this book or encouraging anyone. But because I survived, changed my life and am now thriving, I know it was all for a purpose and a reason. To help you, reader.

I spent a lot of time fasting, crying, and praying. This process was difficult and painful because God was stripping me of all that I had known. It was not just about fighting to get my children back. God was demolishing my past while he re-built me from the inside out. When I was postured to pay attention and hear God, He did not take it easy on me. He was building stamina in me. He gutted me to the core. He made me face very hard truths about myself; about who I was.

If you can not acknowledge the truth about who you are and how you got here, you will not be able to make permanent changes in your life. While I was fighting for my life with my children, God dealt with me about my physical weight. I was perpetually stressed out which left me no energy to tend to my body. Truth be told, I was so consumed with the problems in my life, I did not realize I had gained so much weight. I honestly couldn't see it. I did not pay any attention to it. We can become so consumed with something in our life that we fail to pay attention to other areas of our lives that need attention. When God finally got my attention, he knew that he had to address everything. He will bring every issue to the light while at the same time, correcting with compassion.

It will be hard, but you are growing. I am still amazed at the woman I have become. God kept his promise to me. He promised me that it was okay to leave my children with their father for a short time because it was his will that I would raise them in North Carolina. Only God knew what was ahead for me. Looking back now I can totally comprehend and understand exactly why I had gone through it all.

I am no longer quick to ask God why? I have in fact reached a place of maturity where quitting is not an option for me. I position myself mentally to evaluate or reevaluate things. Giving up is not an option. I now understand that there is a lesson in everything we experience in life. We need to acknowledge the fact that we allowed ourselves to end up in certain situations.

Overcoming

You will know you have grown when you can acknowledge that part of the reason you're where you are is because of choices you made and not because of someone else. I always wanted people to acknowledge their wrongdoings before I could move forward, but many times that didn't happen. That's when I got stuck.

Changing was not an overnight thing for me; nor will it be for you. I can not stress it enough. You are going to have to do the work. You are going to have to learn to manage yourself and hold yourself accountable for your choices and your change.

What does success look like for you? We may have created a false opinion of what success should look like based upon the definition we've gotten from watching other people. My successes may not and most often won't match someone else's. The areas where I know I have accomplished things are now what matter to me. For me, making my bed every single morning no matter what is an accomplishment for me. For years it was not a habit due to my depression that kept me bed bound. For someone else losing five pounds is an accomplishment or small success. My point is don't compare your accomplishments to the accomplishments of other people.

Be your own person. Don't hide your issues because of how other people may react. It is not your responsibility to control how people perceive you. Walk in truth and acknowledge what you need, based on what you want to accomplish, not on anyone else.

I overcame and so will you. My strength came from God. He was and is my power source. My will to move forward and my courage to continue comes from the truth and hope of God. This book is not about pushing a religious agenda. This book came to fruition from a place in my heart of pure desire. Desire to inspire, encourage and motivate. What has helped you through some tough situations may be completely different from what has helped me.

I am being real when I share that it has always been my relationship and constant communication with God in prayer that has helped me keep it together. This is most especially true when I wanted to let go and give up. Your religious beliefs are none of my concern, there is no judgment here. My concern is that you stay in a place where you remain motivated. I want you to know that your life has a purpose. You are here for a reason. There is great value in who you are, including your faults, flaws and inadequacies. I want you to make it to a healthy place in your life where you are thriving and living your best life. This will put you in a position to help someone else someday. It matters to me that you understand that you matter. It took a very long time for me to see the value in who I was; because of that, I consider other people before myself. I lost so much of myself because I did not think I mattered. I didn't understand the value of investing in myself.

Let me tell you how free I am now, and it sure feels amazing! If you are not at your best there is absolutely no way you can be productive in anything. Repeat after me right now:

'I am valuable and I do matter. Who I am becoming means something to me. I will make it a point to celebrate my accomplishments no matter how small. I will continue to acknowledge that I have a place in this world. What other people think about me is not more valuable than how I see myself. I will continue to change, grow, and develop. I will be successful in whatever I set my mind to. I will not allow setbacks to force me to quit or forfeit my purpose. I will continue to learn who I am and where I desire to go in life. I will not stop learning and growing. I will trust my process. I love who I am becoming. I will continue to put my best foot forward and push for greatness in everything I am given an opportunity to be a part of. I will promote positivity in my environment. I will maintain control over my emotions.

My happiness is my responsibility. I will be financially responsible and stable.'

Positive Vibes

Learning to speak positive affirmations over yourself daily
will help keep you in a better head space. Negative thoughts
lead to negative outcomes. Invest that same energy into being
positive and speaking positivity into existence. Every time
you feel negativity, begin to affirm yourself. The previous
paragraph are affirmations I speak over myself. Come up
with your own.

Once you create a safe space for yourself you won't search for
it in other people. You are capable. It is time for you to start
planning for your future. Think outside the box. Anything you
desire is possible. You have to speak life into yourself. I encourage you to write your affirmations down on flash cards and post
them where you will see them a lot.

There will be days when you feel you don't have the strength to
speak your affirmations. Having them posted allows you to read
them even on bad days. Excuses are not allowed on this journey
of self-discovery. Excuses add unnecessary weight to what you
already have going on. The more you grow the lighter you will
feel.

This new place may feel a little uncomfortable at first but don't
worry, you will adjust. Go with the flow. This time you are in a
safe place because of your awareness. That is what will make you
successful. Maybe you have given up on something you desired

to do. Pick it up again. Try again. This time your follow-through is going to be efficient and effective. You can handle the weight of starting over. I know you are ready because you are still reading!

CHAPTER 7

Believe in Yourself

The growth and stability you've developed up to this point will become essential to your process moving forward. I hope you are mentally in a place where you can confidently trust your thoughts and emotions. Believing in yourself means you are conscious of who you are. It puts you in a position to accept who you are and what you are capable of achieving.

This new mindset has changed everything for you. Before your transition, believing in yourself may have been a scary responsibility; committing to a life with chaos and dysfunction. I hope you have rediscovered your voice. It matters. Confidently pronounce life back into yourself. Discover the value of believing in yourself to keep you in a place of constant progression, especially in those instances where your voice is the only one you hear.

Strength From Within

People in your life may not be cheering you on through your recent changes. That is okay. Reach within and pull on the strength and courage that you have developed along your journey to self-discovery. When I was going through my journey of self-discovery, I initially thought the process was heavy. The interesting thing is that the more I told myself I could do it, the easier it became. I had to continue to remind myself of my 'who' and 'why.'

Trust me, I understand it is easier said than done. It will get easier. I used to think that the goals I set for myself were just fantasies. I spoke and acted them into existence. I am no longer living life on cruise control. Once I arrived at the point in my process where I really believed in myself, it felt surreal. Now that I believe in myself it makes speaking life to my heart's desires much easier.

There was a time whenever I opened my mouth, nothing but negativity spewed forth because of the darkness in my life. I had to face the truth. No one likes to be around negativity. Being with me was like standing outside in the rain with nowhere to go. I did not see the good in myself at all. I was sad and de-pressed. That kind of energy is depleting to all around.

I am so happy that is not who I am anymore. I am thankful I can trust what is going on in my life and plan constructively. I am appreciative that I no longer run and hide and allow others to make resolutions for me. I am ultimately in a secure place in my life where I have identified that I am a fighter. I have accepted the fact that the only way I will fail is if I fail to try. I know that I matter and that I have a purpose and a destiny to fulfill.

Unstoppable

If you don't believe in yourself you will believe in what you hear spoken about you, even if it is untrue. The power in believing in yourself promotes sustainability, especially when you step out in faith and go after what seems crazy to everyone else. You become unstoppable because you know what you have on the inside. This desire to evolve in life does not have to be a dream. It can be your reality. You know who you are and where you are going.

Surround Yourself With The Right People

You may become a threat to some. And some people will see you as nothing more than a goodwill project. What I mean by a goodwill project is folks who want to take credit for fixing you. They want to feel like they are your lifeline. It is empowering to them. It makes them feel 'better than.' I had given plenty of people the power to make me their goodwill project. I was weak, wounded and most certainly did not believe in myself. However, I could not blame anyone for the positions that I allowed myself to be placed in.

I am now no longer fighting to sustain relationships with people based upon a lie. I've adopted the motto 'quality over quantity.' I stopped focusing on who isn't there for me. And I turned my attention to who is there for me. This refocusing has allowed me to see reality. The more I accomplished in life, the less I saw or heard from some people. Sometimes people want to be in your life because you are wounded and broken. They are accustomed to helping you. To your needing them. It gives them power in the relationship. As much as they complain about your dependency, it makes them feel good about themselves.

That co-dependent relationship is over for me. I've evolved. I'm still the same person but I don't define myself as 'damaged goods' anymore. No one else is going to either.

Too Valuable For Bad Company

Before my transformation, I claimed I was valuable in secret but not enough to claim in public. Now I know my worth everywhere! I don't need anyone in my life who can't appreciate the value I bring to a relationship. You will need to do what I did, and have the strength to release every person or situation in your life that is not serving a purpose. Some relationships will be hard to let go because dysfunction may have become normal. Sometimes brokenness is necessary to heal properly.

My nana who raised me was very old school. No one messed with her. She was very strict. When I was twelve years old I was invited to my very first birthday party sleepover. That may not seem like a big deal to you but I had never spent the night with anyone who wasn't family. Convincing her to let me go to the party was not the hard part, it was the sleepover that was work. I begged and pleaded. The answer was still a big, fat NO. I had my friend's mom call and ask her if I could spend the night. I thought for sure the answer would still be no but to my surprise, it worked! She let me go.

Lessons Learned The Hard Way

I will never forget this story. The birthday party was at a skating rink and the sleepover was at my friend's house. I was excited to go to the skating rink. I had roller blades at home so I was pretty good at skating. My younger brother and I rollerbladed outside all of the time. When we arrived at the skating rink we picked up our skates and skated for hours. As we were skating, my friend's older brother grabbed onto me. I'm not sure if he grabbed me to keep from falling or what, but I struggled to break free. The next thing I knew I was flying backwards across the floor of the skating rink. As soon as I landed the white watch I was wearing on my left wrist flipped somehow and I felt a pop immediately in my wrist. All of a sudden my wrist and hand started to feel hot. I did not cry because I did not want to embarrass myself. But I knew my wrist was broken.

My friend's mom got ice from the food court and she said I probably just sprained it. She wanted to call nana and I begged her not to. I agreed with her even though I knew my wrist was broken. I told her it was probably sprained and I would be okay. It was my first real sleepover and I did not want to have to go home. I was in terrible pain. My wrist and hand started to swell more and more. My friend's mom ended up calling nana to make sure she knew what happened. I spoke to nana on the phone and she asked me if I was alright. I told her I was okay just a little sore. Looking back, even now, I have no idea how I managed to stay at the sleepover with as much pain as I was in. I have since learned that I have a very high pain threshold.

The next day I went home and when nana saw that my wrist was so swollen and bruised she knew something was wrong. She took me to the hospital where they did x-rays. The x-rays showed what I had already known, I had a broken wrist. Thankfully, she was not upset with me. She felt badly that I had stayed at the sleepover and could only imagine how uncomfortable I must have been.

I had a temporary cast put on my arm and was referred to an orthopedic doctor. When we went to see him, he reviewed the x-rays from the hospital and replaced the temporary cast with a permanent one, which was supposed to stay on for six weeks. This cast only extended to the middle of my forearm. I still did not regret staying at the sleepover.

I was nearing the end of the six weeks so we went back for a follow up appointment to have the cast removed. Once they took it off another x-ray was taken and they discovered the bone had failed to heal properly. The bones in my wrist had fused together and they were crooked. As soon as the doctor mentioned the word surgery I tapped out. I told them I didn't need surgery because I could still use my arm. Of course, nana had the final say. Much to my dismay, she scheduled the surgical appointment.

They put me under general anesthesia. I was completely asleep and didn't feel a thing. When I woke up though the pain I felt told me my wrist had been re-broken. This time the cast was up past my elbow. I went through another six weeks in a cast, which actually turned into a couple of months.

The moral of this story is I was willing to endure much pain and discomfort for a new and fun experience. For me at that time, the good outweighed the bad. I knew I had broken my wrist but I refused to tend to the pain.

Another lesson to glean from this story is the fact that had they not re-broken my wrist to correct the deformity in my bone, my wrist would not be fully functional. I would have been limited in using it. I am a nurse and I need my wrist to be fully functioning. To break my wrist again was necessary so that it could heal properly and I could have full use of it once again.

This is an analogy as to why it is important to break off with some people and situations in your life. The relationship has many deformities that you have chosen to overlook. Once you break all unhealthy connections and set new ones, you will heal properly and be fully functional on both sides.

Breaking Off Doesn't Have To Be Negative

There most certainly will be pain and discomfort during the breaking off process, but once it fuses back together in alignment, it will begin to feel better and stronger. I almost forfeited true healing in my wrist which would have affected my life moving forward.

We can not do life alone. Healthy relationships are important and detrimental to our growth. We all need strong, influential people in our life that will speak truth and light into us. We need people that we trust. Had I not had nana looking out for me, things would have turned out quite differently for me.

Although pain does not feel good. It is necessary to feel it. As you feel, you acknowledge every step along the way. Remember, it is important to identify where you are in your process and to continue to walk in your truth. I want to remind you not to be ashamed of your process. Shame will cause you to hide and deny. You do not have time to draw back. You are finally in a place of power. You are in control of you.

YOU Are Enough

Keep telling yourself that there is power in your process. Continue to remind yourself that you are brave and bold. Tell yourself that there is value even in your insecurities. Every component that makes you who you are matters. Being able to acknowledge who you are overall takes strength and determination. But when you know who you are, you won't look for validation in other people. You will not be disappointed when others don't support or encourage you. You won't need them to because you have already validated and spoken life into yourself.

When you believe in yourself you exude confidence. People tell me I am cocky. I correct them and tell them I am confident because I know who I am and whose I am. I let people know that for me the only way I can fail is if I do not try. We have been taught to fear failure so we won't even attempt to do anything that will require hard work and consistency.

There is something amazing about finding yourself! It's empowering. There have been many things that I have spoken over myself where people thought I was crazy. Truth is, there have been things I have spoken over my life where I scared myself. I honestly believe that the only way I can fail is if I don't properly prepare and position myself for success. At this stage of life, what else do you have to lose? Every time I think about what I didn't get because I didn't believe in myself makes me want to try that much harder now!

Don't Ever Give Up On A Dream

There was a time when I struggled on minimum wage. Paying $600 a month for rent was hard. Mentally and physically I felt defeated. Working long hours making minimum wage while taking care of three children is not easy. I was coming to the end of my lease and did not want to live in the small apartment anymore. The rent was also going up. I started looking for places. I came across a house for rent so I talked to the landlord. She told me the rent was $700 and $50 dollars for the gas bill. It was a three bedroom house with a kitchen, eating area, two full bathrooms and a den. If my rent was going to be more, I wanted to be in a house. The house was perfect but I immediately counted myself out because it was too expensive. I gave the application to someone else who was also looking to move. I didn't even think twice. The gas bill made it too much for me to handle financially. My plate was full enough. How could I add another bill? We ended up staying in the overpriced apartment.

I did not believe in myself and was not ready to fight for a change in my life. I did not do any research nor did I even think to ask what an average gas bill was for that location. I gave up before I even tried. Ultimately, it served as a learning lesson. I learned that at that time I could have actually managed the house and the gas bill in my budget. I let fear and doubt overshadow everything else.

Learn From Your Mistakes

I didn't look at what happened with regret. I took the lesson and learned to ask questions going forward. I learned a valuable lesson about speaking from a place of positivity instead of a place of defeat. Knowledge is power. The more information you have, the better prepared you will be to make wise decisions in your life. It is important to make decisions based upon facts. When you deal with facts there is a greater chance that your decisions will be unbiased.

I have become my own superhero because I believe in myself. I understand the things I desire for my life are all possible. I am now in a position where the smallest things excite me. The littlest changes in my life are major to me. I went through a season in my life where I had to do life on my own. I believe God has allowed people to come and go in my life but the one person I can depend on is myself.

God is my Father. And a good father. I can compare it to when a parent helps his baby when she starts to walk. God has helped me every step of the way. He knew I would be okay. He understood that I would fall and acquire some scrapes and bruises; but ultimately I would be okay. He was confident in what he placed on the inside of me. He knew that if he allowed me to keep hiding in my relationships and needing things to be loud in my life, I would never search for the treasures he placed on the inside of me. Treasures I could only find being still and quiet. Not only would I never find my treasures, but I would never learn how to use them.

When we are quiet it forces us to deal with ourselves. Although I did not always like being by myself, I began to understand it and respect it. God quieting the world around me forced me to find myself. I was able to locate the strength that I had on the inside. I learned to tap into the wisdom that he placed on the inside of me. I learned to become fully functional. I stopped blaming God for the way my life had been and started thanking him for truly never leaving me to myself. From birth until now my life has always been very colorful. I was born a fighter but life just made me feel weak and defeated.

Going After My Dream

As defeated as I was at the time I moved to North Carolina, had I not established some level of belief in myself, the move never would have happened. I had reached a point where I was exhausted physically, emotionally, and mentally. I could either give up or fight for more. I decided to fight. It was time to go after a dream. A dream I had wanted to accomplish for years. It was going back to school to obtain my nursing license. I knew that it was going to be very difficult. I also knew if I was successful it would change my and my children's lives forever.

I knew beyond a shadow of a doubt that God created me to care for people. I knew that I had been given the ability to nurture people and to care for them. I didn't question my purpose, I did question my stamina in pushing myself to achieve my goal to the end. I learned to take each day as it came. I would tell myself at the hardest times that this is what I was supposed to be doing. Failing for me was not an option. At times my fellow classmates thought I was crazy. I would insist I wasn't stopping unless they threw me out of school or God told me it was over.

Nursing school was my hardest but most rewarding accomplishment. Failing a test did not make me feel like it was over, or that school was no longer an option. I refused to allow failing a test to force me into a mindset of defeat. Even though school was hard I was positive that it was for me. Anything worth having is hard. I also reminded myself that when we make an investment in something and it becomes a success, it becomes invaluable. We pay attention to what we've put blood, sweat, and tears into. I had never believed in myself like this before in my life.

I was a single parent going to nursing school with absolutely no physical support. I couldn't let that stop me from accomplishing my dreams of becoming a nurse. My children were 13, 11 and 9. I promise, had I not prayed as hard as I did to make it through school and for God to keep my children safe, I would not be a licensed nurse today. I really had to go hard for my children. I could feel the freedom just on the other side of my struggles. Not only freedom but fulfillment within myself as a woman, mother, and provider. I always told myself being a mother is great but I wanted more for myself as a woman. I am a real example of how anyone can turn their life around.

Nothing Worth Having Is Easy

My life was hard but I also had children with special needs. My oldest son was diagnosed with Asperger's Syndrome. My second son was diagnosed as an asthmatic as a toddler and later diagnosed with Attention Deficit Hyperactivity Disorder (ADHD). My youngest is a severe asthmatic who was diagnosed before the age of one year old. We as a family have faced many challenges over the years but failing was not an option. With every challenge and set back we faced, I managed to find the strength to keep pushing. My life has not always been the prettiest picture, but I've always managed to stay true to myself.

I've never been one to put anyone down because I remember being in a low place in my life where a way out did not seem possible. I want you to believe in yourself.

Everything in life has a place and purpose. Just think if there were speed bumps on the highways. Can you imagine how bad that would be? It's where something good is where it doesn't belong. The fact is, speed bumps would cause many accidents on a highway. Even though they were meant for good. Not believing in yourself is no different. Because we have been stagnant for so long, we may have positioned ourselves in places we should not be. What once was good has turned bad.

Let's recap. Positioning ourselves for success is extremely important. We are walking in faith and not fear. We are trusting the transition and the process because we are thinking differently. Because we believe in ourselves we see ourselves differently. We are no longer waiting for things to be handed to us but are creating opportunities for ourselves. We are paying attention to our relationships, communicating properly and establishing healthy boundaries. We've started to disconnect from unhealthy connections in our lives. We have found our inner strength and have learned that we are our first line of defense.

We've done some soul searching so we can establish our own lane in life. I'm hoping we've also gained security within our own abilities. In life we are only in competition with ourselves. We've learned that disappointment is a part of life. It doesn't mean we should quit or give up. We are confident in our ability to accomplish anything we put our minds to. We are aware it is okay to fail as long as we learn the lesson and keep moving forward. We no longer wait for people to validate us because we are now capable of doing it.

There is a difference between taking a break and quitting. Breaks are necessary. It is okay to take a step back and reevaluate a plan and maybe even make some necessary adjustments. While you are breaking and making any necessary adjustments, be sure to pay attention to yourself and know when you need to retreat. Make time to refresh and be refueled.

The most important point is believe in yourself. It's important to speak life into yourself.

Proverbs 18:21 'Death and life are in the power of the tongue: and they that love it shall eat the fruit thereof.'

I interpret this verse to mean that what we speak will manifest. If we have the ability to speak life why keep speaking death? Being negative is not a viable option if your goal is to live. Speak what you expect and position yourself to receive what you are asking for. Stay hungry for more and always be ready as if you know when your expectation will come to pass. There is a method to the madness. Never wait until you get something to learn how to function with it or take care of it. Wisdom says, prepare yourself ahead of time and do your research so that you are already prepared. You got this!

CHAPTER 8

Go For It!

In my opinion, there is something very satisfying about getting a green light. Like when you're stuck in traffic for hours at a stand still and finally, the traffic clears allowing you to proceed to your destination.

Just like in life, you can have a plan and be excited but you can be stuck unable to move forward. But once you have the clarity and courage to move forward, your excitement catapults to a whole new level, like getting a green light.

I am sure you have taken part in a race at some point in your life. Think about the anticipation that builds up as you wait to start the race. That anticipation is what propels you forward in an attempt to win the race.

It is time to stop thinking and start doing. No more procrastinating! Everything you need to be successful is already inside of you. It was just buried. If you take control of your life you will see results. You will be at your green light for life!

Do you remember the dreams, aspirations and goals that you once had? The things you once craved but lost your appetite and desire for? You're still reading, so I'm hoping you are putting in the work to achieve what you want in life. It is going to be necessary for you to put into practice every bit of knowledge you have gained up to this point.

Your Future Is New

There is something very reassuring about establishing your independence from your past. You no longer have to make choices based upon your past and lower your standards for what you want out of life. Remember, your past does not define you or your future unless you allow it to.

My nana used to say 'everything that glitters is not gold.' Sometimes people are not what they seem. There are a lot of people who have mastered being a public success but a private failure. Behind closed doors, they are a mess but once they step out in the public setting they know how to turn on and off like a light switch. That is why we do not need to compete with anyone else.

Truth be told, we have no idea what it took to acquire what they have or what they had to give up. We need to settle in our lane and stay there. We need to avoid distraction.

You matter. You are valuable, and you do have a purpose. I keep repeating this throughout the book because I want it grafted into your mind and soul. Some of us did not grow up hearing positive affirmations. What we did hear was the exact opposite. I've done a lot of work to come out from under the negativity I have experienced in my lifetime.

You have not only come to the last chapter, but you have also reached the end of a sour season in your life. You have the right to speak and expect everything that you want. I do understand that we all have gone through situations that we did not understand. Situations that caused us to question our worth. Situations that made us want to give up on life. Please don't devalue the things that you have survived even if it doesn't seem as severe as someone else's experience.

New Life

I firmly believe God allows us to experience as much as we can handle. What was hard for me, may not have been hard for you and vice versa. You don't have to match anyone else's struggle to find purpose and value in what you survived.

The enemy meant to kill, steal, and destroy me. When I saw it for what it was, I learned to walk in truth and be transparent. For me, being a woman of faith, it seemed I had to fight to achieve anything. The enemy tried to kill my confidence at an early age. His desire was to make me see myself as weak and vulnerable because then I wouldn't have the courage to fight. For a long time, his plan worked, for many years actually.

You have a fresh start! Knowledge is power. I hope after reading this book you have a better understanding of your 'who' and your 'why.'

Foster the healthy relationships that bring purpose and inspiration into your life. You don't need to focus on who is not in your life but on who is.

If it doesn't uplift, encourage or promote positivity then it is not for you. Stop wasting your time. Don't allow other people to waste your time. We can disconnect in the healthiest way possible. Ending a relationship doesn't have to be awkward and uncomfortable.

Emotions can cause us to communicate poorly. Write your thoughts down prior to having important conversations. When you are looking for closure, write down exactly what you want to express. When you read over what you have written it may also help to see things differently in other situations too.

We are not responsible for what we don't know but we are responsible for what we do know. Take inventory of your life. What are you truly passionate about? Where do you see yourself? Your responses need to be based solely upon what you think personally. It is not necessary to run them by anyone else. Perception is a reality for most people. None of us see things exactly the same.

Trust Yourself

When I made the decision to go back to school after being laid off from my job, I thank God I wanted a better future for me and my children. And I wasn't afraid to go for it. If I would have listened to the people in my life, I would not be a licensed nurse today. Making the decision to go back to school was the easy part. Finishing school and taking the boards were the challenging parts.

One would think trying to better oneself would rally a lot of support. That's not always the case. It wasn't for me. It was up to me to find the strength to trust what was inside of me. I was forced to dig deep and muster up every ounce of courage to get through. I had to allow God to make the necessary connections that were going to be the most beneficial for my success.

Even though I got over not having support, I was still affected by it. It bothered me for a long time. Those same people that didn't support me would say today that they did. From their perspective they did. Sending a quick text instead of calling. Or congratulating me on passing a test instead of asking how they could help with my children. There are not many people that will inconvenience themselves to help someone else.

That is why you need to be all in even if it means being by yourself through it. Unless you desire success for yourself you won't have it. No one is going to desire success for you more than you.

Solid From Within

Identifying healthy boundaries will help you to maintain your focus on your plans. Your foundation has to be solid from within to withstand the winds of life. You need to always be prepared for the unexpected. Don't think you've got a full proof plan. Always prepare for the 'what if.'

Putting yourself in a healthy space mentally is very important because it will allow you to become emotionally secure. I'm hoping you're feeling the difference between where you are now versus where you were before. You have taken the time to discover yourself.

The journey to self-discovery for me has been very emotional at times, frustrating at others, but also exciting too. For example, I was about 23 when I realized that blue was not my favorite color, purple was. I only picked blue because that was my nana's favorite color. The more I discovered myself, the more I realized how interesting I actually am. I am not as basic and simple as I once thought. I was a brave little girl who grew up to be a courageous woman. I acknowledge that surviving my past and continuing to move forward is what makes me valuable. I acknowledge that no matter how weak I feel, I'm actually very strong. I discovered that even though I don't always make the best choices, that doesn't take away from the depth of my intelligence. I learned that just because abandonment and rejection seemed to be a never-ending trend throughout my life, it does not mean I'm not valuable. I discovered that if people have failed to see the value in me, it's through no fault of my own. I discovered that I did not have to be accountable for the actions or reactions of other people. If someone dislikes me and is rude, I do not have to return the favor.

I've also learned that although I was a teen mother, that doesn't make me a failure at life. In fact, because I decided to keep my child and fight to give my children all that I could, that makes me a great mom. I've learned that age most certainly does not define maturity. I figured out that I had misplaced my faith, putting it in man and not God, which is why I was always disappointed. I started directing my faith past people and I learned how God can really make something out of nothing. I've also learned that I did not have to place my comfort and peace of mind in the company of people who made me feel less than.

The most valuable lesson that I've learned on my journey is that I will never compare myself to anyone else. I was created to stand out. There really is power in my words. I need to believe in myself and speak what I want to achieve.

It wasn't just people tearing me down but I had been tearing myself down. I've learned how to encourage myself and speak life to myself. I've learned how to build myself up and speak positivity over every negative thought or word. Through my process, I've begun to see myself through a totally different lens. My lens before was dark. As if I dropped my glasses in black paint and put them back on without cleaning them and trying to see. My vision concerning myself and my life was very distorted and murky. It was almost impossible to think clearly because I couldn't see very well. When we cannot see clearly we have anxiety.

It is okay to not know every single detail. Sometimes the only thing we can do is to prepare as best as we can.

I want you to be encouraged. You may be just starting your journey to self-discovery and if you are I encourage you to embrace every single part of it. Have fun learning about yourself. If you are confident and secure with who you are then you will teach people how to treat you. You will learn to not be in a relationship with just anyone, especially anyone who doesn't understand how valuable you are.

You may be on a journey of self-discovery and need a boost into the right direction. It can be a very intense process if you are completely open to it. It can also be very exhausting. Keep pushing. Don't let a small bump in the road cause you to quit. Make a conscious decision to be in control. Take the time to figure out just what makes you, you.

Fight for your confidence. Fight for stability. Fight to establish peace in your life because you deserve it. I challenge you to not just be okay with the good parts of you, but acknowledge the not so great parts also. My point is, no matter where you are on your journey, you are at your green light.

Nothing or no one can stand in your way anymore. You have taken back your power. Life is about lessons and we will continue to learn, grow, and evolve. Adjust your expectations accordingly. I'm hopeful you will be better equipped to bounce back after disappointment than you had been in the past.

I pray you are much more optimistic about your life and the endless possibilities that are available to you than ever before. For me, it was a euphoric feeling emotionally once I grasped the knowledge of just how much further I could go in life. I was so excited to learn about how many opportunities were still available to me despite the fact that I had previously lacked the courage to pursue them.

You've got this! I wish I could really express how excited I am for you. Because you are reading this book, you have made the conscious decision to better yourself. You are a fighter and not a quitter. It is now your time and your turn to finally leave your mark in this world.

Nothing is off limits when it comes to success in life. Beyond the challenges and setbacks you will experience, remember, a delay is not a denial. Don't rush your process. It is important you learn along the way. If you should ever be faced with similar circumstances again, you will have the wisdom and knowledge to navigate again. Learn the lesson so that you don't have to keep failing tests and repeating grades. There are many people who fail not because they aren't capable or smart enough, but because they lack drive, confidence, determination and will power.

No more hesitating and slowing down. The more now, more you accomplish, the more you establish yourself and the easier it becomes to live the life you never thought possible. I promise, I have been places I never thought possible. I have seen things I never thought I would be able to see. Once I stopped focusing on failed memories of people who walked away or disappeared, God started connecting me with people who were doing life with a purpose for a purpose and on purpose.

He has linked me with people who have become influential in my life. People that push and encourage me to go after my dreams and pursue them with passion, perseverance and drive until they become my reality. Just like writing this book. This is a project that has been a deep desire for years. I did not want to write just to write. I wanted to write something that would affect change in the lives of many people.

Never discount where you are or where you have been. It is all a part of who you are. I have finally arrived at a place in my life where I am not ashamed of my past. You have the power and ability to rewrite your own story. Make sure you are truthful with your past. God's purpose is not to shame you but to deliver you so you can continue to grow. It is no different than why a child is born. A baby can only develop up to a certain point in utero before it will start to develop deformities due to the lack of space and being forced to stay in an environment that no longer benefits him. In order for us to grow, we have to be born. It is necessary to go through the birthing process into an environment that is more con-ducive for the next phase of life. Allow yourself to be planted on the right job, in the right relationships, or even the right place of residence. Don't make a decision that forces you to compare or compete with others; it's just not necessary. From now on, make decisions that are based upon what works for you and yours. Tell me that does not excite you!

Don't forget to affirm yourself daily. Let your speech come from a place of positivity, faith, and pure expectation. You have de-veloped in this womb of life to full term. It is now time to be re-born so that you can grow and maximize in a lane all of your own. Anything new is scary. Identify what you are feeling and know that you control your emotions so they don't control you.

During my journey there were some people who looked at me as if I had my head in the clouds because of how my conversation had changed. I was no longer singing songs of sadness and gloom. I had come to the realization that although I had been through some hard situations in my life, I did not have to be a victim. In fact, I learned that I was a victor because I survived. I came out with wounds, scars, and bruises but I still came out. You will too!

The bigger I made my expectations and the faster they manifested, the more I expected. What is the harm in letting go and taking the limits off of your life? Seriously, doing the work and investing in your process will dramatically change the outcomes in your life.

For me, it took blood, sweat, and tears. Do not settle or become comfortable. Position yourself strategically for the next level. For as long as you have breath in your body there will always be something for you to learn and different ways for you to grow.

If you ever reach a point where you feel as if you can not be taught, that my friend, is when you will stop growing as a person. Don't allow yourself to become complacent and unteachable. Don't expect anything from people that you are unwilling to do for yourself.

As I bring this chapter to a close, I'd like to end it in prayer. My prayer is that you will feel the unconditional never-ending overwhelming love of God. I pray you receive every bit of wisdom that God gave me in writing this book. I pray you will keep this book as a forever reference point. On the days when you are struggling and feel like giving up, I hope you will look back on your notes and the places you highlighted or bookmarked or left a sticky note, and find the encouragement you need to keep going.

Open your heart and clear your mind. There is power in prayer and even more power when you apply your faith unapologetically to your prayers. I want you to read the following prayer and keep it close to you because once you establish a secure connection to your Creator, you will be unstoppable. Many blessings to you as you continue on your journey and stay focused. You are right where you are supposed to be at this point in your life. I love you with the love of God and look forward to hearing from as many people as I can about how this book has touched your life. Like a phoenix rising out of the ashes, it's your time to fly. So fly high!

The Trust To Be Rebuilt

'Trust in the Lord with all thine heart; and lean not unto thine own understanding. In all thy ways acknowledge him, and he shall direct thy paths.' **Proverbs 3:5-6 KJV**

Lord, today I come before you saying, 'Thank you for being who you are. Thank you for your love and patience. You are a God who is great and mighty to be praised. I am not just thankful for my blessings but I am thankful that you love me beyond every fault and flaw. I am thankful that even on my worst days you still call me yours. Lord, I know that I haven't always deserved your grace and mercy. I am grateful Father, that your mercies are new every day. I appreciate the fact that you are merciful to me, even when I do not deserve it. Thank you for seeing the best in me when all I could see was the worst in myself. Thank you, God, for not condemning me to my past but pushing me to fight for my future. Lord, I come before you to repent of my sins. God, I ask that you wash me thoroughly from all of my iniquities, cleanse me from all unrighteousness, and all filthiness of my flesh and spirit. Father, I ask that you forgive me for the things that I have knowingly done as well as the things I wasn't aware of. Lord help me to continue to reestablish my faith and trust in you more than ever before. Lord, I have misplaced my trust in people causing me to abuse the trust that you placed in me. I repent that I have given so much of myself to other people and hid so much of who I am from you. God help me to pull myself together so that I can be successful at whatever you created me to do. Lord give me the strength to not only take the limits off but to keep them off. Thank you for every opportunity that you already have made available to me. Father, thank you for the opportunities that are coming. Thank you for always being a provider and my protector. Lord, your word says that I am to trust in you with all my heart. Lord with every broken, bruised, and wounded piece of me I give it all back to you. I ask that you would mend what I have allowed to be destroyed and even the parts of me that I may have destroyed myself. Lord, I desire to be whole again and to know you. Help me not to depend on my own intellect and my own way of thinking. Lord help my unbelief. My desire is to truly acknowledge you in all that I do so that you will continue to direct my path. Lord, thank you for success. Thank you for loving me enough to correct me. In Jesus' name, I pray, Amen.'

I could not have written this book or achieved what I have without the courage and the power that my mighty God has given me.

Jesus once said, 'Whoever comes to me I will never drive away.' John 6:37

Acknowlegements

I would like to take this opportunity to thank those who have played a very significant role in this projects! I appreciate the countless hours invested into making this book such a success. First and foremost I must acknowledge and thank Ms. Courage Molina. Thank you so much for pushing and encouraging me past my fears and right into my purpose with this book. I also have to acknowledge Kirsten my amazing editor. To my creative team thank you. Alicia Moss and Olivia Heyward you guys really have been so professional and supportive. At times when I may have doubted myself your excitement and enthusiasm gave me the boost that I needed.